Lady Killer

(Book Five of the Confessions of a Chick Magnet series)

by Jenny Gardiner

Chapter One

COCO Lovingston was sorely tempted to bring home the adorable pink teacup pig with the black spots that some cruel person had left in the mailbox at the Second Chances Animal Rescue Clinic where she worked. Her landlord would kill her though, not to mention her apartment neighbors, especially if the little porker turned out to be a squealer. She'd retrieved the pig with the day's mail and hadn't set the animal down for the past hour, instead cuddling and kissing that sweet baby pig face.

As much as she adored animals, her living situation didn't lend itself to taking on a pet. A short time ago, she'd moved back to Bristol, Montana from LA following a disillusioning stint trying to break into acting jobs there. Although she hated slinking home with her tail between her legs, if she were honest with herself, she was happy to be back. She'd spent more years than she'd liked in a too-large city dealing with downright predatory industry types who demanded sexual quid pro quos for jobs. Enough was enough.

If one more rotten man told he she had to give him a blow job to land a pitiful little commercial spot as the "girl with herpes virus" or "girl with joint pain" in a pharmaceutical ad, her head was going to explode. She was damned if she was going to advance her career on her knees. Hell, if she was going to have a career that entailed spending a lot of time bent over, it would be to hug sweet, homeless dogs and cats that people brought into the clinic, thank you.

One condition of her return home, though, was that she would not encamp in her parents' ranch outside of town. It would've been too much of a step backward to live at her folks' place as though she were still back in high school. After being out of the house all these years, she knew her mom and dad enjoyed their empty-nest freedom and besides, she didn't want to deal with them monitoring her every move. Instead, she'd taken a small apartment in town above Vertical Drop, the ski shop on Main Street, and enjoyed walking most everywhere she needed to go. Her best friend from high school, Emma Hamilton, had recently moved back to Bristol, which meant she now had a burgeoning social life. Things were looking up. Now if only she could find a home for this adorable little piglet.

"You planning to do anything other than cuddle that chunk of bacon?" Tippy O'Brien, a tiny sixty-something woman with shoulder-length frizzy gray hair and bright blue eyes, said with a grin.

"Hush," she said, covering the pig's ears. "Little Oink here will get scared."

"I hate to tell you, Coco, but Oink's not going to be long for this place—we don't have the room for a pig right now. We're already at capacity." She frowned.

Coco held the pig up right in front of the director's face. "Look at this little snout," she said, making kissy noises as she held the pig's face between her hands. "How could you ever dream of getting rid of this sweet little nugget?"

"Believe me, I'd bring in ten of them if I could, but we're not set up for pigs to begin with, and she's going to take up the space that several dogs could occupy." She looked at her watch and tapped the face. "Clock's ticking on Oink's time here, Coco. I'm terribly sorry about that."

Coco thrust out her lower lip in a pout. "Give me a day or

Sleeping with Ward Cleaver

"A fun, sassy read! A cross between Erma Bombeck and Candace Bushnell, reading Jenny Gardiner is like sinking your teeth into a chocolate cupcake...you just want more."

--Meg Cabot, NY Times bestselling author of Princess Diaries, Queen of Babble and more

Slim to None

"Jenny Gardiner has done it again--this fun, fast-paced book is a great summer read."

--Sarah Pekkanen, NY Times bestselling author of *The Opposite of Me* two and I'll see if I can find a good home for her."

Tippy nodded. "We'll do what we can, but please, make her adoption your priority."

"Here—hold my pig." Coco passed the pig to her boss, then pulled her long, newly blond hair back into a ponytail. Now that she was back in the area, she'd changed the color of her hair and had it professionally straightened to go along with her new-old life in Bristol. She gave her a wink, her green eyes sparkling, and grabbed the little pig back. "I think I'll be able to do that, no problem."

By early afternoon, Coco had fielded six "no's" and about four "are you crazy's", not to mention "Mommy said I can't" from one little girl. She could barely suppress her failure-to-adopt dismay when in walked a tall, brown-haired man with striking aqua-blue eyes that reminded her of the water at Grinnell Lake in nearby Glacier National Park.

As he approached, Coco was seated at the counter mindlessly braiding the front strands of her hair. She jumped up, her hair falling into her face, and threw on a baseball cap to hide the mess as she greeted him. If only she'd put on makeup and made half an effort to look good. Instead, she'd taken a long run and showed up to work sweaty, looking as if she'd rolled out of bed. So much for making a decent impression on the first good-looking man to step foot into the clinic since she started working there.

"Welcome to Second Chances," she said, ushering him into the lobby. "If you have any questions, I'm happy to help. Are you here to adopt a pet?"

He nodded. "I'm looking for a kitten for my mom's

birthday," he said.

"Oh, fun. Kittens are the best. Has your mom kept a cat before?"

He shook his head. "Actually, no. My father passed away last year and he would never let her have a cat and she always wanted one."

"So sorry about your dad." She frowned. "I bet your mom could use the companionship."

"To be honest, my father was a bit of a tyrant with her—he was an old-school dominant male. Surprisingly, Mom's had a bit of a renaissance since he died. She's got a kick in her step and she's been happier than I've seen her in years."

"Wow," Coco said. "I don't know if that is sad or joyful. I guess the latter."

"Not gonna lie. I'm pretty jazzed to see her so much happier," he said. "I mean, I respected my dad. He was a hardworking rancher. But he wasn't a warm, fuzzy kinda guy. He had a hot temper and short fuse and my brother and I learned long ago it was best to avoid him altogether." He frowned. "We both got out of town as soon as we could and never looked back. Poor Mom didn't have that choice."

"But you're back now?"

"I've been telecommuting since I came back to help my mother settle Dad's affairs and sell off the ranch and all of the assets. It was too hard to do that long-distance. Plus, I'd been living in LA for a while but was tired of the traffic and the whole scene. It's been okay being back in the area. I grew up in Grundy, about an hour away from here. After selling the ranch, I helped my mom get settled in a retirement community outside of town here. There's much more for her to do in Bristol than in dinky little Grundy. There's barely a traffic light in the town."

"Well, I'm a new returnee as well, so it's nice to see

someone else who got stuck returning home unexpectedly." She rolled her eyes.

"What're you in for?"

She laughed. "Right? Like a prison sentence but not really. I'm glad to be back. Grew up here. I, too, was in LA for a while and it turned out it wasn't for me. Happy working with animals of the four-legged variety versus the type of predatory animals I dealt with in the entertainment industry."

"Can I apologize on behalf of the asshole men who did that?"

"Nice of you to offer but not yours to apologize for them." She smiled. "So, before I take you back to the kittens, I have an idea," she said, holding up a finger. Although this felt a bit dishonest because, well, the guy was getting his mama a kitten after all, why not save the life of a cute little black-spotted pink piglet? She led him over to the makeshift pen they'd set up in the kennel area for Oink. "This here's our newest addition to the clinic," she said, scooping up the tiny pig and kissing her right on the snout. "I call her Oink. Someone left her in the mailbox if you can believe it. I like to say she was a special delivery for the day."

He knit his brow. "Someone dropped a pig in the mailbox?"

She nodded. "People suck sometimes. But now she's here and I've got to find a home for her before she goes on the chopping block."

His eyes grew wide. "Seriously?"

Coco dragged her fingers across her throat, sticking out her tongue. "Can't even say she'd be destined to become bacon cause she's too little."

"Well, that's heartbreaking." He frowned. "Except I'm here to get a kitten."

"Did you ever think that a cat might be a bad idea? After

all, cats live a long time. You mom might be too old to care for her eventually. We had a cat that lived to be twenty-four years old!"

He scratched his chin. "Huh… My mom would be into her eighties by then."

"And this cute little piglet would be the perfect alternative to a cat. Just think, no dander to stir up allergies. Have you ever been around cat fur?" She scratched at her skin dramatically.

"It's true. Cat fur makes me itch like crazy. But it's for her, not me—I figured cats are low-maintenance. Don't you just get a litter box and be done with it with a cat?"

"You can train this little porker with a litter box as easily as a cat. And look at this little face." She hoisted the piglet up to his eye level. "Plus, if you need anyone to help watch Oink, I'll be happy to pitch in every now and then."

"A pet pig seems crazy. But my immune system would be happier."

"I hear it's the worst, the itchy eyes, scratchy skin."

"And I get so stuffed up that it's hard to breathe."

"I never heard of anyone being allergic to one of these little babies."

He pursed his lips. "I'm not sure. I mean, a pig?"

"Tell you what—if you have any issues, I'll take her back. But I'm pretty sure you'll adore her. Besides, look at this baby." The piglet batted her eyelashes at him as if on cue.

He heaved a sigh. "Oh, hell, why not. Mom's already turned over a new leaf and gone for the unconventional. A pig would totally fit her new life philosophy."

She scratched her number on a sheet of paper and handed it to him. "Call me if Oink gives you any problems."

Coco decided she deserved a hike after the successful rehoming of the piglet. She was overjoyed—at least the poor baby wouldn't be put down for lack of an appropriate caregiver.

As she closed up the shop, she called her friend Emma, who worked as an accountant in the next town over.

"Dude. Hike. Now."

"Awww, wish I could," her friend said. "I've got to stay late to finish up a few things, so no can do."

"What fun are you? All work and no play makes Emma—"

"Makes Emma an accountant."

"Good point," Coco said. "Although I'm proud of you for having a real job unlike some of us who can't count past our ten fingers and are instead relegated to changing cat litter boxes by the dozens and giving dogs flea baths."

"But you're nourishing your soul, so there's that. Tell you what—meet you for drinks on the rooftop at Harry's after your hike, say, nine o'clock?"

"That would be perfect. I need to be around humans and beer, badly. Plus, I can tell you all about the new home I found for the cute piglet, so mission accomplished for the day."

"That pig you texted me the picture of? You already found a home for him?"

"Yes, to this super cute guy who came in today."

"Huh. I never pictured the forever home for a piglet to be with a hot guy."

"Like only ugly guys take in pigs?"

"I dunno. I mean what would a young dude want with a pig?"

"Chick magnet?"

"News flash: pigs are not puppies."

"Oink's the next best thing."

"You are super weird, you know that? But in all seriousness, does the guy know it's not going to stay tiny?"

"What do you mean? It's a teacup pig."

Her friend laughed. "That doesn't mean it remains the size of a teacup. They grow up to be pigs."

"No kidding? Like big pigs?"

"I read something online one time that people buy them cause they're tiny and cute only to discover they don't stay that size and then they unload them."

"On adoption clinics."

"Yup."

"Oh shit. Like how big is big?"

"I think like three hundred pounds."

"No! That can't be."

"Google it if you don't believe me."

"Crap. I need to tell this guy before he gives it to his mother and she falls in love with it. But if I don't get out hiking now, I'll lose daylight. I'll call him first thing in the morning and let him know he needs to bring it back to me." She switched her phone to her left hand as she scrubbed her right one over her face. "I feel awful."

"Definitely let him know! Before they get attached to the thing."

"Fine. I'm on it. Meantime, see you at Harry's. If I'm not there by nine, send out the rescue squad because it'll mean the grizzlies got me."

"Nothing to joke about, Coco."

"Oh, please. I've been hiking in these woods for most of my life. Has a bear killed me yet?"

"There's always a first."

"Order me a beer—not a bear—and I'll see you at nine."

"Where are you going to be hiking?"

"I dunno. Might go up near the ski resort. Or I might head

over to the trailhead for Iceberg Lake. Gonna pick some berries and enjoy them while watching the sunset."

"Have fun! Be safe. Bring your bear spray!"

Coco laced up her hiking boots and hit the trail hoping to be up and back before dark. Luckily at this time of year, night fell pretty late. She'd have plenty of time. After she parked at the trailhead, she tossed her phone onto the driver's seat—no need to have that along since there was no cell service anyhow. She took a swig of her water bottle, then stuck it onto the side pocket of her pants. That's all she was bringing along—she didn't want to lug anything extra because she was hoping to collect huckleberries along the trails and didn't want to carry anything that might crush the delicate fruit if it banged up against the berry bag. And it was a warm enough day to dispense with her sweatshirt as well. She did attach her bear spray to her waistband, though, because, well, bears.

Maybe a mile past the Iceberg Lake trailhead she encountered an older gentleman sitting on a rock who could not stop coughing.

"Have you got some water?"

He held up his hand and shook his head, but continued coughing as if choking.

"Here," she said, holding out her water bottle. "I won't be walking long and won't need this—why don't you take it?"

He reached for her water and guzzled it down in a flash, then stood up and gave her a big bear hug.

"Thank you so much—I'd been enjoying the bounty of my berry-picking until one got stuck in my gullet." He pointed to his throat. "I thought I was going to choke to death." He offered the remainder of the water back to her.

She held up her hand this time. "Thanks, I'm good. You hang onto that in case you need it again. But you found a good spot for berries?"

He turned and pointed off to the right. "You'll need to divert off of this trail about a mile and there are tons of them, back in the woods."

She held her hand at her forehead to block the sun as she peered in the direction he was pointing. "Perfect. I'll head that way now. Thanks so much for the tip!"

"Thanks for saving my life!"

Coco took off in the direction he'd steered her and soon followed some smaller offshoots from that trail in search of the elusive berries. She'd picked this area because bears frequented it—which meant there'd be prime bear food: berries. She was in competition with grizzlies for the things and they tended to snarf them up for themselves far too often, not that she could blame them. But if she found enough of the delectable berries, maybe she could make a huckleberry pie and bring it out to her mom for dessert tomorrow.

Pretty soon she'd filled her bag with the juicy berries and decided she'd better find her way back onto the trail if she wanted to get to Ptarmigan Falls in the hopes of catching some of the sunset. Although she wouldn't make it to Iceberg Lake, she hoped to get some beautiful color at that popular stop along the trail. But when she started to retrace her steps, she got disoriented. She'd gone off-piste, which meant there were no trail markers, so she tried to see where her feet had recently compressed the overgrowth on the forest floor, but for the life of her, she couldn't tell which way she'd come from. She tried to walk toward the brightness in one direction, figuring she'd reach a clearing, but instead she found herself deeper into the woods without a clue.

She was no rookie when it came to hiking, though, and she knew to keep her wits about her and not panic. She'd be fine. There were plenty of berries in her bag and she'd find her way out in no time. Except that dusk was soon descending, and the forest quickly grew darker. Maybe that "don't panic" mantra was complete bullshit. With the setting sun, a chill soon settled over the forest. Alone, with no sense of direction, no water or warm clothing, and nothing to eat but a bagful of berries, she wondered if she should've dropped some along the way like Hansel and Gretel with the popcorn. Or was it crumbs? What was it they dropped again? Now she'd better hope she didn't happen upon an old woman who wanted to pop her into an oven. Or worse, a grizzly with a hankering for huckleberry pie.

Chapter Two

ELLIOTT Barbour was no sooner out the door and driving down Main Street with a pet pig than he realized he was a damned fool for being talked into adopting a pig, of all things, for his mother. She was going to flip out over it, and not in a good way. Nothing like a little bit of buyer's remorse to kick in when you're bringing home a porcine pet for your unsuspecting widowed mom. He needed to rethink this. Evidently this was a dick-driven decision—after all, seeing that gorgeous blond chick toying with her hair when he walked in had set him on a path to make choices based on how hot she was, not on how appropriate (or inappropriate, as the case may be) the adopted animal in question was.

If he'd entered the animal clinic and a seventy-year-old bald man with missing teeth had tried to dupe him into a pig, he'd have told him no without a second thought. But the way that woman made that kissy-face with the piglet was so damned adorable. He'd have traded places with that pig snout in a heartbeat to get close to those heart-shaped lips. He'd always been a sucker for a girl who loved animals, ever since he was a little kid and his father's farmhand Delilah would teach him about the animals on the ranch. Delilah was the perfect antidote to his cold father, and he learned plenty about farm living from her that he'd never absorbed from his crotchety dad.

But this took the cake. Bringing home a pig—*a pig!*—

when he went in for a kitten, all because he was so easily led around by his dick. He needed to reevaluate his priorities. Or maybe he needed to get laid. It had been a while—at least since he'd moved back full-time to Montana—and he'd not been on so much as a date since then. If all it took was a pretty blonde to lure him into bringing home an unwanted pig, then clearly he needed to rethink things a bit.

Checking his watch, he realized the animal rescue clinic would be closed. He wasn't going to be able to do anything about the piglet tonight. He figured he'd bring it home, try it on for size with his mother, and more than likely make the call to the woman first thing in the morning that he was bringing the thing back. He felt bad about it—he didn't want to see this poor creature's life cut short through no fault of her own, but he also couldn't carry that burden. *A damned pig!* He scrubbed his fingers through his hair. What the hell had he been thinking?

With Oink in the small dog crate he'd picked up at a pet store outside of town, he entered his mom's place through the back door, slamming the door to the screened-in porch as he walked inside her brand new townhouse.

"Elliott? That you?" his mom called from upstairs.

"Ma, come on down. I've got a little surprise for you."

The more he pondered this, the more he knew this was the stupidest idea he'd come up with in years. He heard her footsteps as she padded downstairs. Pulling Oink out of the crate, he held her up under his chin, her face pointing toward the kitchen entryway. His mother knit her brows as she walked into the room.

13

"What the heck are you holding a piglet for?"

"Her name's Oink. It's a surprise—your new roommate!"

Eleanor Barbour rubbed her brown eyes with her fists, then blinked hard, opening them wide.

"Mom? Everything okay?"

She shrugged. "I was just closing my eyes to be sure this wasn't my imagination. Because I couldn't fathom there would be a way that my son would show up with a pig for me."

Elliott extended his arms out for her to take the pig from his hands. She shook her head and crossed her arms over her chest.

"Ma, just give her a chance. Look at how cute she is." He lifted the piglet and held it alongside his cheek like they were a matching set.

"Sorry, not sorry, babe. I lived on a ranch for a long damned time and I am one hundred percent over dealing with farm animals, thanks. Granted we never kept a pig, but I have zero interest in doing that now. Besides, don't you know those little teacup pigs turn into big fat pigs eventually? That's how they end up in animal rescue clinics. Or else on someone's dinner plate as a moist, tender pork chop." She gave first the pig then her son a little affectionate head-scratch. "I know you can't be serious. This is a big joke, right?"

"No, it's not a joke. I planned to find a kitten for you—I know how much you always wanted an indoor cat, but Dad would never let you keep one—and somehow, I came out with a piglet."

His mother burst into laughter that made her graying bob shake. "Oh, honey. I'm afraid to ask, but is it possible a really cute woman talked you into a pig instead?"

He furrowed his brow and pursed his lips. "Maybe."

She leaned over and kissed his cheek. "Perhaps that's a sign that you need to branch out and get away from your old

14

mom and find some companionship closer to your age." She gave him a hug. "I appreciate the kind gesture. I know it's the thought that counts. And yeah, I might be more inclined toward a kitten than a farm animal, so if there's a chance of swapping it out, I'm game."

Elliott shrugged, then tucked the piglet underneath his armpit. So much for his brilliant surprise.

He pulled out the sheet of paper with the gal's number and decided to give the adoption woman a call to set in motion the return of little Oink, but his call went straight to voice mail. Then he sat down and Googled the life span of a teacup pig, only to learn it was pretty much as long as a damned cat. What the hell was he thinking, being led by his dick like that? All of a sudden, a cute little allergy-inducing kitten was starting to sound like the purrfect pet. Too late.

Oh well. Looked like he was stuck with the pig till morning. After a late dinner and an hour of trying to calm down a squealing pig, he at last retired for the night, ready for a good sleep.

But somewhere around four in the morning, he got a call from the team leader of a rescue group he'd started volunteering with that some woman had gone missing from a late-day hike, and he was needed to help spearhead an attempt to find her in the wooded, mountainous terrain.

Even though it was summertime, it got quite cold at night, and beyond the hazards of freezing in the wilderness came the danger of grizzlies, mountain lions, and other predators. He loaded the pig—now squealing yet again—into the crate and headed toward the rescue command center at the fire station to start assembling a search-and-rescue team. Hopefully, they could get this woman back in a matter of hours. The pig would have to come along for the ride.

Chapter Three

WELL, crap. There would be no huckleberry pie tomorrow, that was for sure. That's because Coco had already eaten a couple of handfuls of the juicy berries, the remaining evidence being the telltale purple stains on her fingertips. Now she was going to have to conserve berries for sustenance and hydration. The only pie would be in her dreams. She was kicking herself for having ditched the water bottle, but at least she'd have some liquid from the berries until she could get herself back home tomorrow morning.

Coco knew she needed to stay put until daylight, as uncomfortable as that was going to make her. It was already less than pleasant out. The sun had gone down and the temperature had dropped considerably. What had been a comfortable seventy degrees was inching down to a chilly forty-something. At least, that's what she presumed based on how her teeth were chattering. Through the dense tree canopy, she could make out a sliver of crescent moon, which looked beautiful with Jupiter and Venus nestled in its crook. But it was cold. And she was protected from the elements by only a sleeveless tank and a pair of cargo pants.

Her primary goal was to stay warm—it would be the most important thing to survive the night. Hell, no one would even know she was missing yet, so she had to at least get through the next twelve hours on her own out here. At some point, Emma would know something was off and try to track her down. Hopefully.

The wind rustled through the trees as a screech owl sounded in the distance. She only hoped she didn't start to hear the unmistakable snuffling, throat-reverberating sound of a grizzly nearby. Which would be worse—death by grizzly or hypothermia? It would be a toss-up. At least if a grizzly killed her, she'd live on a bit in infamy—that would make all sorts of headlines.

Ugh. She tried to think back to if she even noticed the weather forecast and realized she hadn't a clue if even a cyclone was due to tear through the park. Not that cyclones tended to strike in her area of the country, but still. Today was nice, but tomorrow could be blustery, cold rain—that's how it was out here in Glacier. She shook her head, trying not to get too far ahead in her thinking. There was nothing she could do to control what was coming anyhow, weather-wise. For now, she had to make some sort of shelter.

Right about now she wished she'd been a Girl Scout, so she'd have earned some outdoorsy-type badges: how to make a fire by rubbing sticks together, how to not get eaten by a mountain lion. She liked the idea of that badge in particular: maybe a picture with a lion with his mouth open wide and a uniform-clad Girl Scout prying his jaws open with her bare hands. But seriously—how hard could it be to construct some sort of buffer against the elements? It was a matter of common sense, creating a little barrier against wind and something with a lot of leaves on it to keep her warm.

She fumbled around in the dark for branches with dried leaves strewn across the forest floor and dragged them to an overgrown bush nearby, which would serve as one wall of her lean-to. It was hard finding her way in the dark as she tried to discover anything that would work. At long last, she built up enough of a bed of leaves to sleep on, then covered herself up with more branches and leaves. Ugh, she was going to need a serious shower after this because the rotting leaves reeked of decomposition. She settled her body down on the ground, grateful there were no venomous snakes in Glacier National Park at least. One less thing that could kill her. And she tried not to think about what lurked nearby that *could* kill her.

How would she know if there was a mountain lion? Once, she'd read that a hiker who was about to be attacked by a lion realized it was there because of the overwhelming smell of cat pee. Of course, a big cat's pee would smell even worse than her last kitty Spunky's litter box. Which made her think of that guy with Oink and that made her feel super guilty. If he wanted to give it back to her, he wasn't going to get hold of her. Then she started thinking about how handsome he was and maybe she should've invited him to go hiking with her so she'd not be alone in the dark shivering with goose bumps skittering up her arms.

At least if they got stranded together they could have held one another close to conserve body heat. Assuming he'd be willing to do that, what with them being strangers. Though what dude would pass up a chance to be up close and personal with any woman who had a heartbeat?

She started thinking about how long it had been since she'd been pressed up to a man properly, and then it made her sad. What if she died out here and never got to be with a guy like that again? What a life wasted it would be. Shit. She needed to get out of here ASAP. First thing she'd do once she got back to civilization would be to call and see if he wanted to meet for a drink. Which she would gladly do except she didn't have his phone number. No doubt by now he, Oink, and his mom were back home, nestled up in front of the television, Oink eating the kernels of popcorn the cute guy tossed toward her intermittently. Perhaps they would have a cozy quilt over their laps, one his mom made for his twelfth birthday, probably baseball-themed. No, maybe it would be wild west, with cowboy hats and cattle and horses. She shook her head; she was already losing her mind.

What time was it? And why did she not bring her phone with her? Oh, yeah, because it didn't work out here. And those stupid berries. But at least she'd know the time. And she could have entertained herself with pictures of her favorite animals from the clinic—she kept a file of photos of the ones she grew most attached to.

Just think—if she'd adopted a dog, maybe he'd be here with her, lying on top of her to keep her warm and saving her from vicious predators. And if she had a phone, she'd have a damned flashlight. *Oh God.* What if she needed to go to the bathroom in the middle of the night? She'd never find her way back to her makeshift bedroom! She was going to have to cross her legs till morning because no way was she wandering off in the dark for even that. This adventure was fast becoming not all that enjoyable. She wanted to go home and sleep under her blanket. Now!

Mercifully, exhaustion overtook trepidation, and the hum of August crickets lulled Coco off to sleep. Daybreak came early when there weren't curtains to keep the sunlight at bay, and Coco could at last relieve herself. Pulling up her pants, she gathered her berries, tried to discern which way the sun was rising, and headed off in that direction.

I should leave a tip for the maid, she thought as she walked away from her forest bedroom. The joke should have made her laugh, but she was in no mood to laugh.

Depressingly, the hint of daylight was but a tease, and soon a blanket of fog enveloped the mountain where she was. She had no idea where she was going and vacillated between staying put and hoping for rescue or embarking on a return to wherever it was she came from before things got dire.

As she sat there for a while, she whistled a few songs out of boredom, though she wasn't a good whistler. She counted to a hundred in Spanish and English, then decided to challenge herself by alternating one number in Spanish and the next one in English, which only served to frustrate her. It was hard to say if she was more irritated at being stuck in general or because she was stuck with nothing to do and no phone to distract her. After focusing her attention on a spider weaving a web for what seemed like hours, and a few insects skittering across the forest floor, she started noticing how many sounds became more acute without life's distractions. A cricket bounded by, and she realized that by tomorrow, his friends would likely be her breakfast, lunch, and dinner for the foreseeable future. The mere thought made her gag.

She was certain she heard water not far off, no doubt from one of Glacier's many waterfalls. If she didn't find water soon, she'd have trouble. Food could wait, but she couldn't dehydrate or things would go downhill fast. She popped two huckleberries into her mouth, resolving to eat one at a time over a spread-out period to preserve her food supply as long as possible.

"What've you got to lose?" she mumbled, failing to realize that being alone in the foggy, cliff-filled mountains meant her answer could be *plenty*.

The sounds led her to what seemed higher up into the hills, which was counterintuitive, but it sure seemed like that was the direction the water was coming from. Frustrated, she couldn't seem to get out of the forest and into a more open space where she could gauge where she was, maybe even see other hikers in the distance she could shout to for assistance. All she knew was it felt cooler the more she walked, meaning she was headed in the wrong direction.

Sure enough, she eventually came upon a small clearing only to discover about a foot of crusted snow that was impossible to walk on without collapsing into it. She'd have hypothermia if she kept trudging through this. But before she decided to turn back, she scooped snow into her mouth to rehydrate a bit. She transferred her berries into all of her pockets, then filled the berry bag with more snow, so when it melted a bit she'd have water to drink. A primitive hiker's water bladder for sure.

She redirected her efforts on a downward slope, still frustratingly fogged in. After walking for what seemed about two hours, the sound of water seemed closer. Yet without a line of sight, she might as well have been wandering blindly in the dark. The terrain was inhospitable, with lots of rocks and pits in the ground, so after a while, she picked up a large branch to use as a walking stick. If she didn't find water soon, at least she could find a clearing where she could more easily be discovered. She'd read about someone who was rescued after using rocks to spell out SOS—that should be easy enough to do. Well, shit. She should've written SOS in the damned snow. That would've been smart.

"Shoulda coulda woulda," she muttered.

She wandered along, trying to be in the moment and focus on the simple joys of listening to birdsong and other sounds of nature. If she wasn't lost, this would merely be another hike in the mountains, and she'd done this hundreds of times. So, she started trying to find where the birds were, looking high up into the branches each time she heard a call and response. She wasn't too well-versed in birdese, so this would be a good way to learn more about them. The fog seemed to thicken and soon, while navigating a rock scrabble, she stepped on a rock that gave way beneath her feet, and suddenly she went toppling downhill, ass over teakettle till her tumbling body came to a sudden stop smack into the trunk of a large tree, and everything went dark.

Well. This was going to make things much more difficult.

Chapter Four

ELLIOTT stuck the pig and a bowl of fruit into the dog crate in a corner of the search-and-rescue office, located above the fire station in town. There were about fifteen volunteers already waiting for marching orders when he arrived. After a briefing, he learned the basic details about the missing hiker: twenty-five-year-old woman, grew up in the area, so very familiar with the mountains. Was supposed to have met a friend for drinks after hiking and never showed up. Didn't answer phone calls. The friend had called the woman's folks, John and Kathryn Lovingston, who had immediately sent their most recent picture of their daughter, but it was a good year old. The mother said she hadn't changed much. They were looking for a woman who was about five feet seven with shoulder-length brown hair. How hard could it be to find her in a million-acre national park?

Their crew had specialists in mountaineering, orienteering, river recovery, off-road driving, first aid, operating a search drone, and even scuba diving (you never know when they need to search for a body in a river), and volunteers were being assigned duties in an effort to find her.

"The subject's car was found parked at the Swiftcurrent Motor Inn," Charlie Kincaid, the man in charge of the search, said of the parking area for the nearby trailhead. "Her cell phone was found on the floor of her car, there was an empty water bottle there as well, and a jacket was on the passenger seat, so it's safe to assume she didn't have anything warm with her since the temperature was in the high eighties and she hadn't planned to be there long, according to her friend who was slated to meet her for drinks around nine. We think she started at the Iceberg Lake trailhead at around five o'clock."

Elliott knew that area—he'd hiked there many times. How hard could it be to find her there? It was a pretty well-traveled trail.

"She was supposedly gathering huckleberries, and the area that people are known to go off-piste to find them was closed after a young adult grizzly charged a visitor who deployed bear spray."

Elliott raised his hand. "So you're not sending anyone out there till the bears have moved on?"

"We're going to monitor things over the next few hours and make that determination. In the meantime, we'll patrol areas free of bears, use infrared from above, and drones to search the difficult areas that are impossible for ground crews to reach. It looks like we've got weather coming in over the next day or two, so things could change quickly. But I'm hoping we've got her back by tonight."

Elliott rolled his eyes. Who was stupid enough to go out there without a phone, water, and a jacket? This woman had grown up around Glacier and should have known better. Sometimes it chapped his ass how careless people could be with these mountains—Mother Nature was nothing to mess around with. Filled with spectacular beauty, these mountains could also be dangerous if things went wrong.

Sometime midafternoon, Charlie took a call that yielded

information.

He clapped his hands and everyone gathered around. "I got a call from a gentleman who said he saw her early in her hike, about a mile past the trailhead. He said he was choking badly after having eaten some berries, and she offered him her water."

"Did she fit the description?"

Charlie shrugged. "He said he was too busy choking to notice much about her, but he said she was about twenty-five for sure. He said he sent her off the trails where he'd found a lot of huckleberries."

"So have the canine units been out that way?" some woman dressed like a firefighter asked.

"Yep." He grimaced. "Took all sorts of crazy contortions, going a whole lot of wrong directions for a good distance, all the way up into the snowpack. But then the trail went dead."

"Near?" Elliott asked.

"A big drop and a crapton of trees and boulders. SAR people couldn't go any farther at that point. Having trouble getting a drone in there, and the other route that we could use has had too many grizzlies spotted for our people to safely get by there."

Oink started making noises and Elliott got up to take her out to relieve herself. He figured if you can train a dog, you can train a pig. Oink's next owner would thank him. Which reminded him—he wanted to call that woman up. Surely she'd answer her phone by now. He pulled out his cell phone and pushed send, but the phone again went right to voice mail. He was growing more and more frustrated with her. He didn't want to show back up at the rescue clinic and get her in trouble with her boss for pawning off an inappropriate house pet. But he also needed to be done with this damned pig.

After the oinker did her business, he scooped her up and

took her back inside. It was gonna be a long day, and he'd have to figure her out later.

Chapter Five

WHEN Coco came to, she was relieved she'd kept hold of the bag of snow the whole way down but wasn't so thrilled when she took a look at her ankle. It was swelling up and sported a fat goose egg that was rapidly changing color. On top of that, her berries were all sorts of smashed in her pockets. She patted her forehead, only to feel a warm, wet spot. She took a look at her fingers, which were smeared with blood.

Well, shoot. This was going from bad to worse. At least it explained why her head was throbbing. She slowly started inspecting herself from the top down, moving her limbs, making certain other remaining body parts were still functioning. To her great relief, everything else seemed to be intact, so she was going to have to work around whatever little issue was going on with her ankle.

After catching her breath, she hoisted herself up and tried to bear weight on the injured ankle, only to yowl from the pain. Dammit. This was not good. How the hell would she get out of here if she couldn't walk? She heaved a sigh of despair. It was late enough that she had to accept that she'd need to give that ankle a little rest before trying to do anything too strenuous on it. She looked around and saw the forest floor was covered in pine needles: she was looking at her very own plush Motel 6, Glacier Park-style.

She grabbed some smashed berries from her pockets and stuffed them into her mouth, then slurped from her bag of melting ice. Crawling on her on her hands and knees, she gathered up the necessary accoutrements to keep warm for the night: leaves, smaller limbs she could snap off of some nearby fir trees, and soon she bedded down for the night, mourning the lack of Advil for her throbbing head and ankle and lamenting the loss of civilization in general.

Hours after she fell asleep, she woke with a start upon hearing coyotes in the distance. Did coyotes eat wounded women lost in the forest? Were they like sharks and could they smell her bleeding head? If there were coyotes, could there be wolves far off? Surely, they'd be licking their chops at a bleeding woman who was out of commission. She sniffed long and hard to be sure she wasn't smelling cat pee and wondered which was worse—death by a pack of wolves, or by a lone mountain lion who might drag her up into a tree where she'd die a long, slow death before being eaten? At least the wolves would cut to the chase and chow down: quick and less painful perhaps?

Coco tried to think happy thoughts. She thought about Oink and wondered how she was doing in her new digs, wondering if that cute man had even given her a second look. Wondered if his mother hated her for having foisted a soon-to-be three-hundred-pound oinker onto her lap. Oy. Or would it be Oynk? If she got out of here alive, she would reach out to the man with the Lake Grinnell-blue eyes and a) take back the pig and b) ask him out for a drink. What with them being two wayward returnees to home base, maybe they'd enjoy each other's company.

She wanted to get back to sleep because at least that made the time pass a bit. Plus you could only worry so much in a state of dormancy. And it might tamp down on her teeth chattering, which probably was a siren call to predators. She clamped down on her molars. No way was she going to serve herself up on a silver platter. She pulled up a branch of pine needles and pretended it was an electric blanket. She remembered one time reading that if you can't sleep, you should take a deep breath and hold it for a count of four, then exhale. A handful of times doing that and *poof!* you're asleep.

She tried to follow those instructions, albeit while breathing quietly. At long last, between the coyote sounds dissipating and the heavy breathing, she fell back into a troubled sleep.

♡

Day three gave her hope. The fog had lifted. Hints of dappled sunshine speared through breaks in the overhead tree canopy. She'd find an opening that wasn't snow-filled so she could stay there and wait for rescue.

She rolled over and tried to get up from being on her hands and knees, and once she put weight on that ankle, she accepted that today was going to suck big-time. Because she was going to have to hobble in pain until something went her way. She stood there with all of her weight on one leg like a flamingo, grabbed some smashed berries and gulped them down, put her lips to her watertight bag of now-melted snow, and gingerly sipped to save the precious fluid. Zipping the bag shut, she hobbled to the closest tree to take care of pressing business. The one upside to drinking very little and eating almost nothing was you didn't have to take care of much in that manner. The downside was she was famished and had started fantasizing about a breakfast of maybe a pound of bacon, but then she thought of Oink and realized she might have to rethink her love of processed pork products.

Before she'd have to worry about that, she had to figure

out how to walk with any sort of ease. Glancing around, she tried to figure out how to fabricate a bandage or splint or something for her ankle. Eventually she gathered up a bunch of vines and leaves, some sticky sap seeping from a tree, and a couple of sturdy twigs to rig up a splint. She glued leaves to the vines with sap and secured twigs on either side, wrapping her clever little natural bandage from the arch of her foot to above the goose egg injury.

Coco stood up, scouted which way made the most sense to proceed, chanted a quick round of "Eenie Meenie Miney Moe," and aimed herself in the direction her finger had pointed. She found two sticks to help ease the way as she walked on her wounded ankle and started the slow slog to God-knows-where.

Coco made a mental note to binge-watch about fifty series on Netflix instead of hiking for the foreseeable future. That is if she ever got back to civilization and had a foreseeable future to foresee. Instead, right now, her ankle throbbed and her head pounded and her stomach growled and her parched throat wanted more than the meager sips she was allotting herself to conserve what little water she had left. And she wanted to cry. But she soldiered on and finally, she saw the curtain of trees parting in the distance, and in its stead, what looked like a high Alpine meadow with late-summer wildflowers and views. If someone were still searching for her and if they were using a drone or a helicopter, maybe she could be found.

She hobbled on her sticks and scanned the area for rocks, limping to anywhere she could find some and tossing them all till she had assembled a healthy pile. Using the rocks, she set about spelling out her message in three large letters: SOS.

Through a combination of tossing and lugging, she had the letters spelled out about twenty feet tall in an hour. Thank God she didn't have to write a huge diatribe or she'd have died trying. She noticed in the distance the smoke from wildfires curling into the late afternoon sky, creating a haze. At least there was no sign of wildfires near her—so common in Glacier in the summer and they spread like, well, wildfire. She was having enough trouble without worrying about that. She hoped all the helicopter resources weren't being used toward putting out fires and at least one might be scouring the horizon for her.

Exhausted, she sprawled out on her back and drifted off to sleep as the sun gave way to a twilight sky. She hadn't even prepared herself for a cold night and was rudely awoken by splashes of cold water on her face. Rain. Crap. The good news was she could open her bag and collect drinking water. The bad news was she'd probably turn into a chunk of ice by morning if she didn't protect herself. But she didn't want to go far from her rescue message. She decided to scavenge for a handful more rocks and created a stone arrow pointing toward the forest line, hoping they'd take the hint and save her there.

For the time being, she opened her bag wide and tried to collect as much water as possible, keeping her head tilted back and her mouth open wide to refresh her palate while she waited, then retreated to the nearby woods to try to keep from being saturated. Later as darkness descended, Coco had a good cry, ate what remained of the damned berries that had lured her into this endless hell to begin with, and crafted a woodland bed for yet another night away from her life. She eventually drifted off to sleep with tears trickling down the side of her face, feeling more convinced than ever she'd never get back home again.

She woke to sunlight and the *wub-wub-wub* of helicopter

blades cutting through the mountain air. She could hardly contain her elation and hobbled as fast as she could to the clearing, where she jumped on one leg and screamed over the noise as the chopper almost blew her down. And then it disappeared. Which was when despondency kicked in. She was starving to death. She had a finite amount of water left and even if it rained more, precipitation had the double-edged sword of being her salvation and doom, so she couldn't even wish the hours away hoping for more rain as that would mean she was also hoping she'd freeze to death, drenched to the bone overnight.

Out of the corner of her eye, she noticed a grasshopper. It was then she knew she'd reached the nadir of this hellish experience. Because she knew she needed the protein that this horrifying critter could provide her. She slammed her hand down over it, cried for about ten minutes over what she was about to do, plugged her nose with her thumb and pointer finger, squinted her eyes, nearly hyperventilated, then dropped the thing into her mouth, screaming as she did it. The texture was a bit like sticks and hay in her mouth as she tried to not chew but chew, all while screaming because, well, she was chewing a fucking cricket!

Sadly, her cricket munching efforts were for naught, because she no sooner tried her best to gulp it, even stroking her finger along her throat to encourage the muscles to cooperate, but her psyche was having none of it and she began to dry heave. She rolled onto her hands and knees as her body rejected the idea of her nutritionally sound breakfast and soon up came cricket bits along with whatever digestive juices had joined in the protest. And she was certain an antenna was stuck in her teeth. If she'd thought the low point was eating the cricket, puking it up was a further step down in the pecking order. She rolled over onto her back, tears streaming down her face, which was flushed and sweaty from the effort. Could life get any worse?

It was then she was certain she heard the sound of humans… right before she passed out.

Chapter Six

BY the time Elliott arrived for his volunteer shift on the morning of the fourth day of the search, he was rather discouraged—he knew the statistics were not in their favor at this point. The vast majority of lost hikers were found in the first twenty-four hours. Most of the remaining ones by day two. After that, the chance of being found decreased considerably. It bummed him out. Even if she had been a complete idiot for going out there unprepared, he hated to think of her suffering alone in the woods, afraid, hungry, cold, thirsty—thoroughly deprived of everything one needs in life.

He'd dragged Oink along with him again as she was becoming an unofficial mascot for the rescue volunteers. He figured if she gave them something to smile about, he'd go along with it. Even though he was ready to throttle the woman who foisted the piglet on him—how dare she ghost him like that? He'd been so busy working rescue in the dispatch center that he didn't even have time to return to the animal rescue clinic to unload the thing. Although he had to admit, he'd been pleasantly surprised that Oink had been sleeping through the night. This morning he even had to wake her to go to the bathroom. That wasn't so bad. In the house, she followed him around everywhere, which was sort of cute. He was starting to like the little porker.

The radio crackled and he focused his attention on it.

"Our subject was spotted from the sky. We have a team

on their way now to extract her."

Those in the room breathed an audible sigh of relief before breaking out into applause. Finally, everyone could return to normalcy, and—assuming they got her out without a problem and she was healthy—the missing hiker could finally return home. It would be the better part of the day before they got her off the mountain, so until then, the volunteers would wait till they knew she was in good hands before accepting the good news. For the rest of the day, Elliott remained at headquarters communicating between teams.

Late in the afternoon, they had word that the rescuers were within an hour of having her back to civilization, so he grabbed Oink and headed to the site so they could watch the SAR team bring the woman to the waiting ambulance—he'd heard she had an injury and needed to be seen by medical professionals. This being his first rescue since coming on board, he wanted to see the person they all worked so hard to save. He got to the trailhead and soon the group showed up, their patient strapped to a backboard, her leg in a splint.

She was bedraggled. Her hair looked like a coat of fur from a runaway collie that had been lost for months, matted and tangled and sticking up all over the place. He didn't envy her that first encounter with a hairbrush when she got home.

Her forehead sported a slice and crusted blood that had dried into her hair. Her pants would be almost funny if it wasn't so sad to fathom what she'd gone through: huge splotches of purple stained either side of her crotch and where the side pockets of her cargo pants were—no doubt remnants of her huckleberry collecting; and her knees were earth-blackened. Her lips were swollen from dehydration and sun exposure; her fingers were stained blue from berries, and what looked like a combination of tearstains and vomit were smeared across her gaunt face. She even had some crazy Tarzan-devised

35

contraption involving vines looping up her ankle. Man, she looked rough.

All of a sudden, she glanced over at him as they were preparing to transfer her to the waiting ambulance.

"Oink?" she said, in a raspy voice, knitting her brows as she looked at him.

"Huh?" Elliott cocked his head, confused.

"Oink," she repeated.

"I'm sorry, I'm not quite sure what you're saying to me. It sounds like you're saying what a pig says."

She squinted and shook her head in a "no duh" way. "Of course, I am. Aren't you Oink's new dad?"

His eyes widened. Oink's new dad? Not hardly. "How do you know about the pig?"

She pointed at herself. "I'm me."

He nodded slowly. "Yeah, you are you." He wondered if the woman had suffered some sort of head injury, what with that gnarly gash on her head.

"No!" she wasn't able to raise her voice much but she seemed agitated. "You adopted Oink from me!"

Elliott's jaw dropped as he started to process what she was saying to him. She was the same damned woman who lied to him about the pig? This ding-dong who meandered off into the wilderness as if she was picking wildflowers in a meadow? In an instant, all the empathy he'd mustered up for her seemed to fizzle away. This woman—what was her name again? Coco something or other?—was nothing but trouble.

He wanted nothing more than to unload the pig on her once and for all, but that wasn't an option. Instead, he shook his head and turned and walked away.

Chapter Seven

COCO was starting to feel like a new woman. After several days in the hospital, she'd returned home for some TLC from her parents for a few more days until she was stir-crazy enough to insist she'd be fine on her own and promised she'd not go off on any wilderness treks for the foreseeable future.

All she wanted was to feel normal again, and being home like that was making her feel like a damned shut-in. The gash on her forehead wasn't so bad once it got cleaned up. It had been too late for the doctors to stitch it; she figured the resulting scar would be her badge of survival. Ish. The doctors had put her in a walking boot for the sprain, which was an inconvenience but better than having to deal with crutches, so she would manage.

Coco had made plans to meet Emma for drinks at Harry's—only a week or so after their original planned get-together. She entered the building and grabbed the elevator to the rooftop. There would be no climbing three flights of steps in her condition. As soon as she stepped out of the elevator, she spotted Emma who rushed to hug her.

"You are a sight for sore eyes," Emma said, sizing her friend up.

"Dude, we saw each other when I was in the hospital. And at my folks' place."

"Yeah, but I'm not gonna lie—you looked like shit in a suitcase, and I was worried for your welfare. You'd lost too much weight and your eyes were sunken and, I mean you looked fierce and not in a good way. Today you're starting to look human again.

"Glad to know I was looking inhuman before."

"You know what I mean. You're back among the living. Let's drink!"

They sat down and ordered beers and nachos, but not without the waitress asking for her autograph.

"What is up with people treating me like I'm a reality show celebrity or something because I got lost in the woods and then was found?"

Emma tucked her curly brown hair back behind her ear. "Right? We are in a weird culture. Any sort of fame gives you street cred. Maybe you need to land a book deal and make a fortune."

Coco rolled her eyes. "More like I could write a report for teacher: 'What I learned on my summer vacation.' Starting with 'Stay on the trails. Bring your damned phone because even if it doesn't have service, it has a GPS tracker. Don't give your water to strangers even if you think it's a nice thing to do. Bring rain gear. And a tent. And a house. And a toilet.'"

They both started laughing. "And don't take rides from strangers."

"Honey, that was precisely what I *did* need!"

She shrugged. "Yeah, I know. But I had to throw in the one Momily I could come up with for good measure." She took a swig of her beer. "So, you're feeling good?"

Coco nodded. "When you think you're going to die because no one can find you, pretty much every day is the perfect day once you've been saved. I feel great. Tippy insisted I stay away from work for two weeks, but I'm starting back on Monday, and I'll be ready to. I'm kind of bored."

"Might as well enjoy the R and R while you can."

"Trust me, I've been indulging in Netflix and lounging on my sofa. That is when I'm not curled up beneath my goose down comforter on my comfortable Tuft & Needle mattress relishing every moment of warmth and security. I think I could stay in bed and never leave it again."

"Newfound appreciation for the simple comforts."

"You don't know the half of it."

"So… I know you're not planning on hiking anytime soon…"

Coco shook her head. "I know I've got to get back up on that horse sometime soon, but for now my ankle is an easy excuse not to do that. I'd be lying if I said I wasn't afraid to. But I know I can't be a weenie about this. Besides—this is where I grew up. I've been in those mountains my whole life. I screwed up, made strategic errors, learned important lessons from it, but I can't run scared forever. Can I?" She winced.

The waitress delivered their nachos and a few people stopped by to welcome Coco back to civilization. She felt super weird being the object of all this attention.

"So, have you talked to your rescuers since they saved you?"

Coco pursed her lips. "Honestly it's been kind of weird. I mean, I'm super grateful for what they did, but I'm also so embarrassed, I almost don't want to face them. They must think I'm such a horrible person for having wasted all of their time."

"Oh, honey." Emma laid her hand on top of her friend's. "You shouldn't be ashamed at all. People get lost in the woods all the time. Experienced mountaineers, even. You know that guy who disappeared last year? He left his dog in the car and went out for what seemed to be a short hike and was never seen again. He knew what he was doing! But things happen that are beyond our control sometimes, and if anyone understands that, it would be people who have dedicated their lives to rescuing people!"

Coco heaved a sigh and sipped her beer. "I dunno. Ya' think?"

"I don't think. I know. And I have an idea." Emma pulled out her phone and typed in something. "Look. I knew I'd seen something about a fundraising event for the rescue squad—it's next Saturday night. There's going to be food and drinks and even a silent auction. What say you go to this thing—I'll join you as moral support."

Coco scrunched her nose. "Yeah, but there's something else."

Her friend arched her eyebrow. "Seems pretty straightforward to me."

"You see, the day I disappeared, remember that pig situation?"

Emma nodded. "You got that back, right?"

"Unfortunately, I didn't. I was going to call the next day, and, well, you know what happened then."

"Oh my God. So that guy was stuck with that pig that is going to grow into a monstrosity?"

Coco threw a chip at her. "It's a cute little piglet."

"For now."

"Why didn't he just take it back to the clinic?"

Coco shrugged. "Hell if I know. I mean, I have a theory."

"Oh Lord. Can't wait to hear that."

"Well, it's kind of why I'm particularly embarrassed."

"Do tell." Emma scooped up some nachos and crunched down on them.

"So I had a bazillion voice messages from him on my cell phone. They got progressively nastier, starting with the first night and continuing all week. Until I was found."

"He didn't know you were the missing hiker?"

She shrugged. "I've seen the posters still hanging in places in town—I guess my mom gave them a fairly outdated picture of me. For one thing, it was old. For another, I had brown hair back then—before I went blond and straightened it. And the other thing is I looked pretty damned amazing in that picture—it was at a film premiere and I had my hair and makeup professionally done and my hair was in an updo. In other words, I looked nothing like me."

"So the you we know and love—slovenly, sweaty from being fresh from a run, no makeup—was the you he met at the animal rescue clinic?"

She nodded. "To make matters worse, I gather that he worked as a rescue volunteer all week, and probably never had a chance to return Oink. So first off I unload a dud pet on him, then because of my irresponsibility he couldn't even bring it back and was stuck caring for it, and to add insult to injury, he was stuck spending his week helping to find me, not knowing it was me, mind you. So, when I was brought down off the mountain, a whole bunch of the volunteers were there at the ambulance cheering my safe return—"

"Kind of them."

"Amazing. They all gave up their busy days and nights for me!"

"Which is why we're going to this thing."

Coco held up a finger. "Not so fast," she said with a sigh. "So, I wasn't exactly at my best that day. If you thought 'slovenly me' was bad, I was more like dire straits Barbie at that point. Not like I had a mirror—thank God—but I saw the pictures that were in the paper the next day. I know you saw them too. I looked like something the cat coughed up."

"And… you're not going to the fundraiser for the people who saved you because you looked like shit?"

Coco's eyes widened in alarm. "Oh God, no! That's not

41

why!" She motioned to the waitress for a refill.

"Then what is the deal?"

"Well, he was there waiting. With Oink tucked all snugly in the crook of his arm. It looked so adorable, by the way."

"Yeah, so he was there."

"And I said something. About Oink. And he was confused because he didn't know it was me. He thought I was hallucinating probably."

"I guess it wasn't the prime time for him to hand it off to you?"

"Not so much. But worse still was once he started putting the pieces of the puzzle together, he gave me this super dirty look and turned and walked away. No words, no nothing."

The waitress brought their beers and they both took a fat swig at the same time.

"Wow," Emma said. "That doesn't bode so well."

"Tell me about it."

"Well did you try to call him back? You said he left all sorts of voice messages in your mailbox."

"Yes! I called him like ten times. I was super polite and apologetic and, I mean, what else could I do? I still don't know who he is or where he is and I mentioned to Tippy that the guy might be bringing the pig back—I even offered to take it myself when I left messages for him to get him off the hook. But so far, no pig, no guy—I don't even know his name—and that's why I am too much of a wuss to go to that fundraiser."

Emma sat for a moment before speaking. "I have a plan."

Her friend rolled her eyes. "Last time I followed a great plan of yours, I ended up in jail for stealing a goat."

Emma waved her hand. "First off, it wasn't a goat. It was a ram. And it was the school mascot for our sworn enemy school in college."

"Whatever. It was some sort of cloven-hoofed ungulate.

But I ended up in jail overnight on a hard, concrete floor with about fifty women in various states of inebriation and had to pay a five-hundred-dollar fine."

Her friend laughed. "Besides that, have I ever steered you wrong?"

"Given the opportunity, I trust you would do so without batting an eye."

"Have faith, grasshopper."

Coco blanched. "Don't ever say that word again in my company."

"Faith?"

Her friend frowned. "No. the icky insect name."

"Not following what you're saying."

"Because I didn't want to die. I ate a grasshopper. It was the worst experience of my life."

Emma started laughing. "Oh, honey, your virgin cricket ingestion? Sounds hideous!"

"I don't know if it was a cricket or a grasshopper. Just something icky and, well, icky. And it was worse than hideous. I couldn't even get it down. I started dry-heaving and I very well might have been in a pool of my own puke when they found me in my weakened state."

"Okay, so no more swarming, crop-destroying insect references, but know that my plan is gonna set it all straight."

Chapter Eight

ELLIOTT was feeling guilty. He'd kind of started to enjoy the darned pig. Which was crazy because he was *not* keeping a pig.

He'd met up for drinks a few days after the rescue with Joe Walton, an older local man who was a fellow volunteer he'd befriended.

"You got a girlfriend?" the man had asked.

Elliott shook his head. "And I'm not looking, either. My last girlfriend ditched me for the guy she swore was merely a good friend, and that was after she'd reassured me about a thousand times over the course of a year. They're married now."

Joe grabbed a handful of popcorn at the bar. "You know you have to get back on the horse."

Elliott laughed at the metaphor. "Trust me, the riding part, I'm all for, it's the relationship thing that holds no appeal."

Joe laughed. "Well, that too. And it requires no hand-holding or double dates. Just go out and pick someone up. Don't you have an app for that? I hear that people your age are using something called Tinder for one-night stands."

Elliott laughed. "Yeah, the hookup app. Only I kind of feel squeamish about using that in such a small town. Plus I don't know how long I'm going to be here. Strange as it seems, it would almost be easier to pick up a woman the old-fashioned way."

"You mean get drunk at a bar and fuck her in the

bathroom?"

Elliott's eyes opened wide. "You mean you did that back in the day?"

Joe held up his hands. "I'm not that old! I've still got kids in high school."

"Sorry, didn't mean to suggest you were old."

"Besides, I know as well as you do a man's got needs."

Elliott frowned. "And yeah, those needs are decidedly not being met. I haven't been laid in so long I can't even remember the last time."

"A nice-looking fellow like you?" He looked around the bar. "And no prospects in all of Bristol?"

Elliott shrugged. "Well, I had high hopes for a brief period." He reached for his beer and gulped a swig down.

"Why didn't you go for it?"

"Well, you know that pig I was bringing in to the rescue headquarters?"

Joe nodded. "Yeah. Everyone kept rubbing its head for good luck when they showed up for a shift."

"Yep. Well, turns out I'd gotten that for my mom at the animal clinic the day that girl disappeared." He reached for some popcorn. "I planned to give it to my mom to cheer her up—she's recently widowed. I went for a cat, but the girl working there talked me into that damned little teacup pig."

"Did she tell you it was going to grow into a full-blown three-hundred-pound hog?"

Elliott choked on the popcorn and his new friend patted him on the back to help clear his breathing passageway. "Is that true? My mom claimed the same thing. But it's a miniature pig."

Joe nodded. "Miniature now. But not forever. Don't you know that little things grow up? And baby pigs become big pigs. Didn't your parents teach you about the birds and the bees?"

"Of course, they did, but they neglected the bit about the piglets and hogs."

"You were saying about the girl with the piglet?"

"Well, this makes things even worse. First, she pawned off the damned pig on me. And my mom about birthed a cow when I showed up with it. She said after spending her life on a farm, the last thing she wanted to deal with was a farm animal."

Joe nodded. "Can't say that I blame her."

"The girl scribbled down her phone number and said if my mom didn't want it to call her. Which I did. And then she never returned my calls. The rescue operation unfolded and I didn't even have time to get back to that place Second Chances to return the pig during regular business hours."

"Which is why you brought that thing in with you."

He nodded. "And I kind of took a liking to it. I'd given half a mind to hanging on to her. But now I can't keep a pig that's going to weigh that much!"

"Good chance there are better places for her than in a single-family home, that's for sure. But what's this got to do with finding yourself a hookup?"

Elliott shrugged. "The girl who pawned off the pig was kind of cute," he said. "Blond, hair pulled back in a ponytail. No makeup—which is a plus to me. I hate when women have their faces all caked with cosmetics. She seemed kind of fun and charming and had a smokin' body. When she gave me her number, I thought maybe she'd want me to call and we could have drinks or something."

"Or something." Joe made air quotes and grinned. "Is that what they call it now?"

Elliott laughed. "So, like I said, I called and called to no avail. And then when I went to meet the crew bringing back the lost hiker, it turns out they were one and the same."

Jenny Gardiner

Joe's eyes opened wide and he whistled long and low. "No shit!"

"Yeah. I don't think you were there at the ambulance. But Oink and I were, and she was looking all sorts of awful on that stretcher and her voice was raspy. She started talking to me and mentioned Oink. I was confused because she looked nothing like the girl at Second Chances."

"I saw the pictures in the paper—she looked more like a homeless woman."

"On meth maybe."

"Trying to be charitable."

"Understood." Elliott drank some more beer. "I was kind of already annoyed. I mean what we knew about her, she was kind of irresponsible when she went on that hike. And all the resources it took to save her. And the whole misleading pig situation."

"Don't tell me you yelled at her."

He pursed his lips. "Worse. As soon as it dawned on me who she was, I glared at her and turned my back and walked away."

"Well now, that's no way to get yourself a hookup."

"Tell me about it."

"Have you talked to her since? After all, don't you have to return that pig?"

"She's called me back, returning my voice mail, about twenty times. But I've ignored them all. I mean, not like this could go anywhere. Too much stuff there, you know?"

"Hell, man. Since when did that get in the way of a good time. Have you never heard of makeup sex?"

Elliott laughed. "We're not even in a relationship, so that isn't even a thing for us."

"Yeah, but you were mad and you let her know it. Now's your chance to clear the air."

Elliott shook his head. "Too much time has passed. I ignored her attempts to contact me. If I reached out now and then came on to her, she'd see right through that."

"So? What if she does? She can always say no. Or maybe she'll have warmed up to you, knowing you had a hand in saving her life. You never know."

The waitress brought them their hamburgers and they took a few minutes to eat.

"You think I should reach out to her and what? Tell her I'm sorry I was a jerk?"

"That's a damned start."

Elliott shrugged. "I don't know. I'll think about it."

"Maybe now's the time to do what all good men do and let your dick think about it for you. Then you'll do the right thing."

They laughed, but Elliott knew he wasn't that kind of guy. He figured the window of opportunity with her had closed and he wasn't going to throw a rock through it to open it back up again.

Chapter Nine

"AND the blue-eyed guy never brought that cute piglet back here?"

Coco had returned to work and was trying to be sure Tippy hadn't missed something.

"I think I'd have noticed if a pig showed back up here," Tippy said. "But am I ever glad to have you back!"

"Awww, you missed me! I was worried you'd fire my ass after I didn't show up for work the next day."

"Are you kidding?" Tippy grabbed a stack of newspapers and started changing out the bottom of the cages. "You're the best thing that's happened to this place since I came along." She gave her a wink.

"You sure know how to make a girl feel wanted, Tips." Coco started pulling up the dirty paper as her boss placed the clean sheets down. "Am I wanted enough for you to give me a raise?"

"Now don't go getting cocky on me, hon. Love you, but can't pay you."

Coco thrust her bottom lip out. "Was worth a shot. At least I didn't get my pay docked for a bad adoption."

"I take partial credit for that one. I pressured you into getting rid of it." Tippy paused. "I mean, with good reason. We've got no place to handle a pig here. But still. It wasn't fair to you to feel so responsible for finding it a home suddenly. Fact is, you did a great job of it!"

"Yeah except it appears the guy was pissed at me."

"He's over it by now, don't you think? After all, we haven't seen the whites of that piglet's eyes."

"Nor her squiggly little tail." Coco thought back to how cute that little nug was, all tucked into her dad's arms when she saw them. At least she thought it seemed cute. Maybe she was hallucinating at that point. They had given her some painkillers by then, so she wasn't quite herself.

"I say let's stop worrying about that pig and see if we can find some homes for the litter of stray puppies that came in while you were gone last week."

"It's a good thing I live in an apartment or I'd be bringing home one of everything in this place."

"That's cause you have a big heart. That's what I like about you."

"Gosh, Tippy, you're gonna give me a big head if you don't stop with all the flattery." She grinned.

"I was worried we were going to lose you out there in the mountains." She washed her hands then grabbed a stick of gum from her desk drawer and popped it into her mouth. "Figured I should tell you how much I like you now that I have the chance to do so."

Coco walked over to her boss and pulled her into a hug. "That's the nicest thing anyone's ever said to me."

"Chances are it's the last time you'll hear something that soft come out of my mouth, so enjoy it while it lasts."

"That's okay—I'll use it as a protective shield against next week."

"What's next week?"

Coco reached for a puppy and pulled it close to her chest, twirling her finger around its tiny ear while she talked. "Emma is making me go to the fundraiser for the rescue squad."

Her boss lifted a brow. "And?"

"And I'd imagine that people there have low regard for people like me who put them at risk. I mean, I already sent a nice thank you, along with some of that good chocolate from Ginny's store—you know the stuff?"

Tippy rolled her eyes back like she was in heaven. "Orgasmic, that stuff is."

"Well, it was the least I could do after what I did. I also included a case of local IPA, because, well, beer."

"I can't imagine that even one of them thinks anything but good things about you, sweetie." Tippy started filling water bowls with fresh water while Coco followed with food.

"I know at least one person there who has no good feelings toward me."

Tippy knit her brows. "Impossible." She swept her hand up and down in front of Coco. "For one thing, look at you. You're so damned cute. No one hates cute people. And for another, you're so young and thin and that makes people want to take care of you. I bet they'd all fight to go rescue you again."

Coco laughed. "Not so much. But I'm telling you, there's a guy who hates my guts there. He's the one who adopted Oink."

"Hate's an awfully strong sentiment."

"Fine. Dislikes intensely."

"I don't know. The day he was here wasn't he lingering for a while? My bet is he has the hots for you."

Coco shrugged. "Well, even if he did, that only goes so far. I'm afraid I exhausted my hall passes with him."

"What makes you think so?"

Coco proceeded to fill her in on all that had transpired, setting the puppy down as she finished her story.

"I don't buy it for a second." Tippy wiped her hands against each other. "I think he has a thing for you, but now he's scared."

"Scared I'm gonna go get lost in the woods." She laughed.

"Scared because he blew it. And too chickenshit to admit it."

"I wish you were right. Because I remember him being pretty good-looking. Those eyes—*mmm mmm*." She made one of those sounds you might make when you're eating a good piece of fried chicken.

Tippy waved her hands in the air. "You young people and your hormones. I say go to the fundraiser next weekend and pull him out of that corner he's boxed himself into. Sure beats staying at home watching reruns."

"You know there are a million things you can watch on TV without ever watching a rerun for the rest of your life, don't you?"

"I prefer reruns, thank you very much."

Coco sighed. "You honestly think I should go there tomorrow night?"

"Can't hurt, might help. Could even land yourself a good-looking guy."

"It's not all about that, you know."

Tippy looked up at her from lowered lashes. "Uh, yeah it is."

Chapter Ten

ELLIOTT was about to call it a night. Which was sad because it was Friday night and not even ten o'clock. But he had nothing going on and was kind of tired anyhow. Maybe this was a sign it was time to move on. Figure out what he wanted to do now that he'd figured out what he didn't want to do, and move on and do it. His phone dinged with a text from an unfamiliar number.

"Meet me at the End Run in fifteen minutes."

Huh. Weird. Who the hell was this? He typed that in and sent it.

"Don't worry. You'll be glad you did. Hurry and get here."

Well, his curiosity was piqued and he knew he had no enemies who would be there waiting to slit his throat in a dark little biker bar on the far side of town. What the hell—might as well go see who it was. It beat going to bed like an old grandpa. He put Oink to sleep in the crate, brushed his teeth, and headed off to the bar.

The loud murmur of a Friday night crowd hit him hard when he opened the door to the bar. Elliott definitely needed to get out more often—he was so unused to being in a social environment with other actual people that even a seedy bar seemed like a life upgrade. When did he become a hermit? He held the door for a pretty woman about his age with long, curly hair who seemed in a hurry to leave. Maybe he should've stopped her, offered her a drink. Which would be fine *inside* a bar, though kinda weird when the woman had her feet out the door. Nah.

As he looked around, he had no idea who in here would have texted him. Until his eyes landed on a woman sitting alone in a both, listening to the fiddler on the small stage playing some bluegrass number. The missing woman. Coco. It had been her! He went back through his phone log and compared it to the number the message was texted from and sure enough, it was she. But what? Why now?

Not wanting to appear overexcited, he casually made his way toward the table, stopping first to grab two beers at the bar. He navigated his way through the crowd, out of her line of sight, and then rounded the corner and slid into the booth.

"You rang?" he said, plunking down both beers. Sitting right next to her, he turned to face her and cocked his brow.

"Ack!" she jumped as she saw him and held her hands up as if it was a stick-up. "What the what?"

"I got your text."

"What are you talking about?"

"You told me to meet you here. You just sent it. Surely you can remember something that recent. I know you hit your head but—"

She shook her head. "My head is fine, but I'm super confused about why you're here."

"I got a text from you about twenty minutes ago asking me to meet you here. Of course, I didn't know who was texting me until I got here and saw you, and then I compared your texts to the"—he squirmed for a minute, remembering that he'd never bothered to answer her many voice messages—"um, er, the voice messages you left me."

"The ones you conveniently never replied to?"

His face became warm. "Guilty as charged."

"Sorry, but I didn't send you any texts. I don't know where

you got that from." She redirected her gaze to the band, ignoring him.

He pulled out his phone and opened up his messages to the one in question. "See, here." He pointed at it, then at the number. "That's your phone number, amiright?"

"Yeah well, I don't know what happened. Maybe I was hacked—" She pulled out her phone and looked at her sent messages, then frowned. "Why, that dirty little witch."

He squinted at her in confusion. "Everything okay?"

"No, it is not okay," she said. "My sneaky, dirty, rotten friend set me up against my wishes. I didn't send you that text—she must've gotten hold of my phone when I went to the bathroom and sent it. And then slipped out when you got here after telling me she was going to the bathroom."

"Your friend—is she about yay high?" He held his hand up. "Brown, curly hair?"

Coco grimaced, throwing him the stink eye. "Were you in cahoots with Emma?"

He squinted. "I don't even know who Emma is. I just held the door for someone leaving when I walked in who fits that description."

"You're going to tell me you were sitting at home, minding your business, and you got this text supposedly from me and voila, like that"—she snapped her fingers—"you dropped everything and came running?"

He frowned. When she put it like that, it made him sound like a pathetic little lapdog. But, uh, yeah.

"I *was* home alone—and bored—when I got the message. Mind you, I had no idea who sent it, but it sounded intriguing, so yeah, I did drop everything. But I didn't run, if that matters." He grinned at her. "Does it help if I tell you I was relieved when I saw it was you?"

Her face softened. "You were?"

He nodded. "Very."

"But I thought you hated me."

"I don't hate you at all. I don't not hate you either. Well, that sounds not good. Let's just say I, well, I felt conflicted."

"Conflicted, why?"

He sighed. "I don't exactly know, now that you ask me. I guess I was annoyed about the pig. And you refused to call me back—"

She held up her hands. "Uh, news flash. I was otherwise occupied."

He put his hand on his forehead and shook his head. "I know, I know. I know. I mean, I know now. But I didn't know then. All I knew then was that I needed to get rid of the pig and you were nowhere to be found. And then the call came in and I couldn't even find a moment in the daytime to slip away to take the pig back, and the next thing you know I'm stuck with this thing. Like a stuck pig. Ha ha."

Her mouth curved up in a half smile, reminding him that he liked her smile, even as weak as it was at the moment. It made him want to elicit a true smile from her.

"Why didn't you call me back?"

He took a big drink of his beer and closed his eyes. "Because I'm weird. Because I was exhausted probably, with the emotional fatigue that goes along with volunteering with a search-and-rescue group. And because I was stuck with a pig. And the person who was supposed to save me from the pig had ghosted me. And because I kind of was annoyed that you went off in the woods as if you didn't know any better and it left us all to figure out how to freaking save you."

She nodded. "I knew it. I knew you blamed me for that."

"It's not a 'blame you' thing. If anything, it's a reason I need to rethink my motives for doing this type of volunteer work. The last thing anyone involved in search and rescue does

56

is blame the person who's gone missing. We all know what you—the missing one—is suffering through. You're scared and tired and lonely and cold and thirsty and hungry and miserable. But then, this logic kept kicking into my head that told me you did it to yourself. Which wasn't logic at all. It was me being an asshole. Because I honestly don't—and didn't—blame you. But then when I saw you, it kind of messed with my head. You were you! Both the missing person and the pig girl! And it just—I mean I just—I mean, I don't know. I froze emotionally. Which is lame of me because when I met you the day I wanted to get my mom a kitten, I desperately wanted to muster the courage to ask you out, but then instead, well, here we are."

"Here we are indeed." Coco drank her beer and rested her chin on her hands. "All because of a sneaky setup by my friend. Remind me to never speak to her again."

He shook his head. "Please don't do that on my account. I'm happy she did this because I'd never have had a chance to meet up with you again, all things considered."

"Though you could have just shown up at the shelter." She swigged her beer.

"Except that I got my chickenshit on."

Coco spat out the beer. "Is that a term?"

"More or less."

"So, should we talk?"

"About?"

"About your thinking I failed the entire search-and-rescue team when I went into the woods, for starters. And about how I stupidly pawned a pig on you that will become a giant farm animal before you know it?"

He turned to face her even though they sat mere inches away from each other. The warmth of her body was palpable from such a close distance. If he wasn't such a pussy, he'd lean in and kiss her. But he was so afraid it would lead to him getting a fat slap across the face and never seeing her again. "What can I do to prove to you I don't hold any ill will toward you regarding your disappearance?"

She shrugged. "I suspect that's on me. I feel guilty about what happened. I did know better and figured it was a short hike and I'd be fine. In all honesty, I did at least bring water along, but I felt bad for the guy who was choking."

"How could I judge you on that? You shared all the water you had with a stranger."

"And the pig, well, I didn't know much of anything about pigs. The pig was so teensy, it never crossed my mind how huge it could be one day! I figured it was like those teacup dogs. Have you ever seen a teacup Maltese? My old boss had one and it was the only thing I liked about him. Anyhow, I never would have pawned her off on you if I knew! My boss was pressuring me to find a home since we weren't equipped to care for her. I'm terribly sorry about that."

"What say we start again." He reached out and shook her hand. "Hi! I'm Elliott Barbour. What's your name?"

"Coco. Coco Lovingston. But I guess you knew that already, considering you had to save me."

"Three cheers for the search-and-rescue crew," he said, smiling. "The world would be worse off without you in it."

Just then the band started playing a song Elliott knew from his childhood. "Care to dance with a guy who actually doesn't hate you?" He slipped out of the booth and extended his hand toward her.

Coco reached for it as she got up. "Why, I don't mind if I do."

It was then that he noticed the boot on her foot—having forgotten all about her injury. "Crap, Coco, I'm sorry. If you can't dance, I understand."

She shook her head. "I'm super light on my feet. You won't even notice I've got it on. Come on."

They walked to the tiny dance floor and wedged themselves in between a small handful of other couples. He reached for her hand and gave her a little spin, pulling her toward him as the band played Bill Monroe's "Good Woman's Love."

Elliott leaned in toward Coco's ear. "This was my mother's favorite song when I was a child," he said. "It always makes me smile because I remember her singing it around the house."

The dance floor was so small it was hard to move, which wasn't such a bad thing, pressed up to her as he was. Of course, if he did much more pressing toward her, things were going to get real hot, real fast. He thought about what he and Joe had discussed. In most cases, he wasn't exactly a hookup kinda guy, but then again, what would be the harm of it? Not that this was where it was going, but if it did…

He guided her so that they were on the outside of the group, not all hot and sweaty with the rest of them, and he could feel her relaxing into his arms while the singer crooned on.

They stayed that way for three more songs, with her soft breasts pressed to his chest, her hips notched to his.

"You are pretty light on your feet, considering you've got that injury," he said.

"Must be all that running I do. Keeps me moving even with a little roadblock."

"No doubt running from all the guys beating down your door to spend time with you."

Even in this dark room, he could tell that she blushed, which he found charming.

"Trust me, there's been no door pounding since I moved

back to town."

"Then there are a lot of foolish men in Bristol. Either that or blind."

He pulled her tighter and pressed his nose to her fragrant hair, fragrant with hints of citrus and vanilla.

"You know I had no freaking idea you were the missing woman," he said as he gazed at her. "The picture your mom provided looked nothing like you."

She laughed. "That was my sophisticated LA look. Not who I truly am but who I was pretending to be."

He pressed her head toward his chest. "I like the real you just fine." He could hardly believe the turn of his luck in a few short hours.

The band took a break, yet they stood there, entwined, on the dance floor.

"You want to get out of here?" He hoped against hope she would.

"Like nobody's business." She gave his hand a squeeze, which told him all he needed to know.

Chapter Eleven

COCO was torn between wanting to kill Emma and wanting to thank her. On the one hand, death by a thousand paper cuts could be the chosen murder weapon. Only because she kept no other weapons, other than a butter knife, which would do as well. Something that would be long, slow, and drawn out— that would make her think long and hard about her crimes of meddling in her friend's life.

But on the other hand, she was about to get out of Elliott's car and go into his house and if left to her own devices, she knew what that would mean. After all, she'd been through a long, dull, dry spell. Maybe this was the perfect time for a sudden warm front to move through and clear the air. And she'd owe it all to her sneaky friend's machinations.

Coco and Elliott held hands but said nothing as they walked up the path to his front door. He fumbled with the key and forced the door open. When they finally stepped inside, he guided her toward him and leaned over to kiss her. Coco wasn't sure until that very moment that she even planned to do just that, but the minute his warm lips pressed to hers, she was all in. For the same reason she didn't know why she cared what he'd thought about her with the pig and the getting lost in the woods, she knew she wanted to be with him. Something about him resonated in a way no other man had. She opened her lips and welcomed his tongue with hers, coaxing him to explore, their tongues twining as her pulse quickened.

With his hands almost tentatively placed on her sides, he seemed to be holding back. Taking the lead, she reached for the hem of his T-shirt and scrambled to lift it between them as quickly as possible so as not to break the spell. Once she got it over her head, she stood back for a minute to admire his broad chest and immediately ran her fingers through the dark hair there as she trailed them along the contours of his torso, slowly inching toward that happy trail below his waist.

After seeking her nod of approval, he tugged her sundress over her head, leaving her in panties and one beat-up cowboy boot and that godawful walking boot. She knew she was half-sexy, half hospital-chic, so she leaned forward to pull back the Velcro strips and kick off the confining footwear. Better one naked foot than one like an old granny. He stood back and took her in, his eyes wide, his mouth curving into a sexy grin. He looked like a wolf surveying his next meal. Then he bent over and scooped her into his arms, carrying her only about ten feet till he set her gently on the nearby gray sectional sofa.

He pulled off the cowboy boot and settled himself on top of her, the hardness of his bare chest pressed up against her bare breasts, the hair tickling her nipples. When he pressed his mouth to hers again, this time his hands roamed along her torso, coursing along her hips, beneath her arms, and cradling her face as he kissed her tenderly. Shifting, he trailed his fingers down toward her breasts, where he stroked featherlight touches everywhere but her nipples, where she needed him most.

She tried to nudge his hands there, but he continued to tease her as he drew his tongue over her lips, along her jawline, and up toward her earlobe, licking and nibbling as he went.

Coco moaned, urging him on, and soon his tongue trailed down her throat as he licked and nipped her naked flesh. At last, his lips encircled her nipples and he pulled them into his mouth, sucking hard while his tongue flickered the tips. Coco thrust her hips toward his, encouraging him with the flow of her hips and the groans she couldn't help but utter.

Her hands fumbled for the button of his jeans and soon she released the button and zipper, then slid her hands in to work them off his hips. Though she needed to feel him hard against her, he clearly had other plans and shifted his body lower, kissing and licking his way down her belly. When he reached her panties, he slid his tongue beneath the band and Coco about died with anticipation. With one hand, he tugged her panties off and with the other nudged her legs apart as he admired her splayed out on the sofa. Coco felt so exposed but so turned on all at the same time. And even more so when he stroked his fingers along her wet folds, a path his tongue then followed, licking up one side and down the other as his fingers glided inside, toward her wet center.

"Fuck, Elliott, that's so good," she murmured, thrusting her hips toward his eager mouth and fingers.

Looking down, she linked eyes with him as he circled her clit with his tongue, an action so fucking hot she couldn't stand it. Her breathing became labored and her pulse was pounding in her ears as he licked and sucked her toward the climax she was barely holding back. When he hooked his finger to find that perfect spot inside of her and sucked hard on her clit, the dam burst inside, her pelvis pulsating in waves, her clit throbbing in the aftermath.

She lay there for a minute as her body recovered, then looked down at Elliott, wearing a broad grin.

"You." She pointed at him. "Here." She pointed toward her pussy.

He arched an eyebrow. "You sure about that?"

"After that little tease? Are you kidding? Hurry, please."

He lifted off of her and pulled his jeans and boxers down,

then grabbed his wallet, pulling a condom out. Coco pulled it from his hand, tearing it open with her teeth as she admired his huge cock, swollen and waiting for her. She leaned down and cupped him in her hands, dragging her tongue across the head of his cock as her hands encircled the girth, stroking him gently as her lips settled on him and she began to suck. Elliott thrust himself into her mouth and they established a rhythm while he ran his fingers through her hair. Finally, he pulled back and let Coco roll the condom onto his hard length. She pushed him onto his back and climbed up his body to mount him, lowering herself onto his cock as they both moaned in unison at the amazing sensation of their bodies joining.

Coco leaned her hands against Elliott's hard torso for leverage and lifted herself off of him, only to glide back down, his huge cock filling her up. Soon she picked up the pace as he helped her along, thrusting upward as she settled over him and taking a nipple into his mouth. Although she didn't think she could come again so soon after that orgasm, she felt the stirrings deep inside as she rode his cock and he sucked on her tits, pulling another climax out of her as he buried himself deep inside. Groaning hard, he released his seed in wave after wave of ecstasy. Coco ground herself against him, wringing everything she could out of the orgasm before she collapsed against him, spent.

She could barely imagine why it had been so long since she'd last done this with a man. And she decided then and there it was time to make a habit of it.

Chapter Twelve

HOLY fuck. That was *in*-freaking-*sane*. How had he not had this woman in his life before now? Who knew he'd been missing out on the best sex he'd ever had? He wasn't sure if he was going to be able to move for the next ten hours, his body was so spent. But after having sex two more times before falling asleep in the wee hours of the night, Elliott knew it was worth it, even if it rendered him in a catatonic state.

Somewhere around dawn, he remembered pulling Coco into a spooning position, her back to his front, and as he opened his eyes, he couldn't help but fantasize about fucking her this way, so he reached down and began stroking her clit with one hand while playing with her nipples with the other. He nestled his cock up against her bottom and groaned. Thank God at some point Coco had announced she was on the Pill, and because they'd both been free of partners for what seemed a lifetime, they'd decided that his lack of additional condoms shouldn't get in the way of their fun. So, he could organize a sneak attack on Coco that she'd be happy to wake up to.

As soon as his fingers were slickened from gliding along her moistened folds, he pressed his cock to the notch of her body and gradually began to slide inside of her, his hands secured at her hips. Coco moaned and turned her head over her shoulder to connect her mouth with his as he slowly thrust in and pulled out, the friction of his cock sliding into her body making his balls ache. He played with her nipples as he pressed as deep as he could to seat his cock and held it there, savoring the warmth of her wet body enveloping him. But when Coco's fingers met his to play with her swollen clit, the pressure built and he needed to move, so he began to thrust hard as his balls tightened up and the release was so close. Two more hard thrusts and he shot his come deep inside of her as she unraveled, her pussy tightening on his throbbing cock.

This he could get used to.

They both fell back to sleep until the soft squeals of a piglet broke the early morning silence.

"Oh my goodness, Oink!" Coco said. "I forgot you had her here!"

"You want to do the honors?"

"Sure."

"Just grab her out of the crate and step out the back door. She'll go down the steps and come back up when she's done. Be sure to put some clothes on so the neighbors don't see you naked. I want to savor that all for myself." He kissed her hard.

"I think it might be kind of fun to tease them, don't you?"

He rolled her over and pressed his body to hers. "You might start a war, between old man Griswold next door and that new young co-ed grad student on the other side." He'd seen the cute, curvy woman—Tammi, wasn't that her name?—a handful of times since she moved in a few weeks ago. Of course, she was always with her boyfriend, an obvious deal breaker, which was why Elliott hadn't bothered to pursue her.

She raised her eyebrow. "A girl?"

He shrugged. "If I was a girl and I saw you naked, I'd want to fuck you."

She laughed. "Not sure fucking is what two girls do together, but I appreciate the vote of confidence. If anything happens, we'll let you watch."

"Oh, honey, if anything happens I'm joining in."

She shook her head. "Cliché male fantasy number one."

"With good reason, duh."

She pushed him off of her as the little pig squealed louder. "Stop while I take care of the little oinker."

Still naked, she scooped the piglet up if only to tease Elliott—and gave Oink lots of little kisses as she took her outside.

When she came back in, she put the piggy down. "You got something to feed her?"

"There's a bowl of cut-up fruit and vegetables in the fridge—you can put her in the crate with that and she'll be fine for a while."

He walked into the kitchen as she was bent over, searching for the pig's food.

"But you'd better hurry because I can't look at you like that without a command performance."

"You perv," she said. "Me feeding your baby, and you just thinking about sex."

"Make that me thinking about burying my cock inside you as you lean over the kitchen counter, your tits pressed to the cold granite while I reach around and bring you to climax with my fingers. As I come inside you again, both of us feeling my come as it seeps out of your pussy, you shudder through the last of your orgasm."

She put the pig into the crate with her food and waggled her ass toward Elliott.

"It seems you've given that a lot of thought."

He shrugged. "Yeah, while I fantasized about the woman next door rubbing one out as she ogled your sexy-as-hell body." He came up behind her and began kissing her neck. "How could I think of anything else."

She bent over and pressed her breasts against the kitchen island, her naked ass in clear view, and grinned over her shoulder. "Your wish is my command."

"Oh my God, Coco, you're killing me." He approached her from behind, rubbing his hardening cock up and down the seam of her ass, his fingers playing in her still-wet folds. Coco spread her legs wide and he made quick work of sliding into her from behind yet again. He let his fantasy take over, imagining Tammi licking her breasts, taking her nipples into her mouth, alternating rubbing her slick pussy then blending her juices with Coco's. Maybe he'd bend her over next to Coco, sliding into one warm pussy and then the other. Fuck, he was going to blow his load into her any second at the thought.

With his hands clasped at her waist, he pounded into her hard, imagining it was Tammi, this time with Coco's mouth on her wet pussy, licking his cock as it slipped out of her and pressed back in. Holy fuck, he was going to come hard. His knees weakened as he plunged himself into her.

"Oh, Tammi, fuck!" he yelled as his come spurted from his cock, filling her with wave upon wave of his warm seed.

He felt Coco tense up. "Who the fuck is Tammi?"

Chapter Thirteen

"LET me explain."

Combined, they were perhaps the three most bullshit words in the English language. Coco hadn't slept with that many men in her life, but of those she'd been with, not one had ever called out the name of another woman while his penis was buried deep inside her. This was a first and not in a good way.

She stood up, Elliott's Tammi-induced semen still dripping from her body, as she fleetingly struggled with how to react. Tammi. Tammi! What the hell?

"Please, Coco, let me—"

The thing is, Coco sometimes could act impulsively and if ever there was a time to act impulsively, it would be after a man called out another woman's name in ecstasy while fucking you. So, she did what any other self-respecting, naked and vulnerable woman would do: she slapped him.

The crack of her hand meeting his face resonated in the kitchen, but she had no plans to stick around to hear any other sounds, certainly nothing uttered from his damned mouth. She turned on her heel, gathered up her clothes, still strewn across the living room floor, threw on her dress, her boot, strapped on that idiotic walking boot, grabbed her purse and shoes, and hightailed it out of his place. He was still spluttering some sort of nonsense, stark-naked, when she slammed the door behind him. Luckily it was two blocks to her place, so she walked as fast as she could, cutting through an alley to preclude him finding her if he came looking, and beelined for her home.

Tammi my ass.

Originally Coco was going to kill Emma. Yet when things seemed so great with Elliott for a few hours, she wanted to thank her instead. Now, though, she was back to wanting to kill her and immediately pulled out her phone and hit send the minute she stepped into her apartment to verbally ream her friend.

"I take it as a good sign that you waited until now to call me?" her friend said when she answered the phone.

"If you ever so much as fantasize about playing matchmaker for me again, I promise you I will strap you down, then drive masonry nails beneath each of your nail beds, one finger at a time, and I will do so with my Bose noise-canceling headphones so that I can't hear you crying out in pain. Is that clear?"

Emma cleared her throat. "Well. So. Ummm." She cleared her throat again. "I take it this means things didn't go according to plan?"

"According to plan? What was the plan, pray tell?" Coco's ankle was starting to throb so she hobbled over to the sofa and plopped down. "Was the plan to humiliate me? If so, I'd say it was spot-on."

"I'm sorry, but I have no idea what you're talking about, Coco. I was trying to give a little push to you two because it was so obvious you both needed it."

"Oh, maybe I needed it," Coco said, aiming her thumb toward her chest. It wasn't as if Emma could see her anyhow.

"But clearly that jerk was all about adding to his stable of fillies."

"Stable of fillies? What does that even mean?"

"It means that stupid me threw caution to the wind and decided to have sex with a two-timing dirty dog."

"You slept with him? Coco! Yay you!"

"Not 'yay you'! Did you not hear what I said? He's a lying, cheating, two-timer!"

"I cannot imagine that is the case. Calm down and start from the beginning, so we can suss this out."

"Suss this."

"Now, Coco, let's come down off the ledge and discuss this like grown-ups."

Coco started to sob. "I don't want to. I was all excited and happy, but then he went and ruined it all."

"I'm sorry, sweetie," Emma said. "But maybe there was a misunderstanding?"

"Uh, pretty sure calling out another woman's name in the heat of passion is not a misunderstanding but rather a royal fuck-up."

Emma gasped. "No!"

Coco nodded into the phone and cried some more. "He did."

"That seems crazy. Maybe you heard him wrong?"

"'Oh, Tammi, fuck'? You think he actually said, 'Alabammy, fuck?' Or perhaps 'My Cousin Sammy, fuck'? Nah, I think it was 'Whammy, bammy, thank you mammy, fuck.'"

"Hmmm." Emma paused. "Okay, so that does sound a little bit damning. But there has to be some explanation for that. It makes no sense."

"Of course, there is. There's some woman named Tammi and he thought he was having sex with her." Coco slapped her

71

hands together like she was cleaning off dirt.

"Did you ask him?"

"Hell no, I didn't ask him! I slapped him across the face and grabbed my clothes and hightailed it out of there."

"You slapped him?"

"Uh, yeah."

"Okay, can we maybe back up? What happened before all of this? You seemed to indicate it had been going well."

"Because I was an idiot." Coco sighed.

"Let's not devolve into self-loathing here. Again, let's backtrack through the night and see what happened to get you here."

"You mean on the road to Tammi?"

"Coco—"

"Okay, fine. So you deceived me and he showed up, and at first, I was mad but then we started talking and he was super nice—"

"Just like you thought he was at the animal shelter."

"Yes. Before he thought I was a jerk."

"I can't believe he thought you were a jerk."

"He was mad at me for getting lost."

"Perhaps he was concerned about you. And I don't think rescue people get mad at the people they're trying to rescue."

"All right. It's true. He ultimately felt bad that he was mad. So we talked. And enjoyed each other's company. And we danced. And then he invited me to leave with him, and I gladly agreed to go."

"Now's when things get juicy."

"Well, yeah. Until they didn't."

"Continue."

"Okay fine, but this is going to be fast. We went back to his place and couldn't keep our hands off each other and had wild monkey sex and I was kind of falling for the guy."

"So, what was the Tammi thing all about?"

"I took the pig out to go to the bathroom. He warned me not to go out in a state of undress. Didn't want to excite the neighbors—some old man on one side, and some young woman on the other."

"Oh, so he's got a little kink in him?"

"Huh?"

"He's imagining you and some hot chick next door going at it?"

"That's a hell of an extrapolation, Emma. Going from me taking the pig out to the backyard to pee while I'm naked to him fantasizing about girl-on-girl sex?"

"Any idea what the name of the girl next door is?"

"I have zero interest in finding out."

"Wanna bet it's Tammi?"

"I don't care if it's Tammy Wynette. It makes no difference. And even if it was Tammi, clearly he's got a thing for her."

"Instead of leaping to conclusions, why don't you do some sleuthing and find out?"

"Like knock on the neighbor's door and ask her if she's doing Elliott Barbour?"

"Elliott Barbour…" Emma said in a whisper. "That's got a nice ring to it."

"Oh no you don't, you nosy thing," Coco growled. "Stay out of this, would ya?"

"Why, I wouldn't insert myself into your private matters. You know that."

Coco knew nothing of the sort and soon hung up on the conversation, afraid that her friend was indeed bent on meddling into things, which would only make it go from bad to worse.

Chapter Fourteen

"ELLIOTT Barbour here," he said, answering his phone, hoping against hope that it was Coco calling to apologize for jumping to conclusions. He'd left her many messages over the past few days but she refused to talk to him, so what was he going to do?

"Elliott? This is Emma Hamilton. I'm good friends with Coco."

He took a deep breath. "Look, she got it all wrong."

Emma started laughing. "Of course, she did. Which is why I'm calling you. It's my fault you two hooked up, so I'm going to give the two of you the nudge you need to fix this silly mess. But first, you have to promise me there's no woman named Tammi in your life."

"Believe me, it was all a stupid thing that had nothing to do with anything. I feel like a complete idiot even discussing this, let alone with Coco's friend. But I'm serious—it was only a stupid screw-up on my part."

"Lemme guess: something to do with a neighbor and your fantasizing about her and Coco going at it."

Elliott could feel his facing turning red. "Um." He drummed his fingers on the counter.

"It's okay, We're all friends here. Hell, I once had a sexual fantasy about having sex on stage with Michael Bublé, so who am I to judge."

"Michael Bublé, eh? In front of a large audience?"

"Packed house. I've got an exhibitionist streak a mile wide."

He broke out into laughter, then held his hands up in surrender. "Okay, you've figured me out. I mean, not that I wasn't focused on Coco, but I guess my mind wandered a little bit after our conversation and, I'm not gonna lie, what guy wouldn't be all over that like white on rice?"

"Yeah, I know. Male Fantasy 101 stuff. But now, we've got a freaked-out Coco who we have to persuade to believe this."

"What's in it for you to straighten this out?"

"Honey, I'm just the good Samaritan who was happy to see my friend get together with a guy she obviously wanted to get together with."

"She did?"

"Of course she did. Only she handled things in a, well, ham-handed way." She laughed. "Sorry, needed to insert a pig joke in there."

"No apologies needed. By the way, I've found a rancher who'll take her."

"Coco? That seems a little drastic."

He kind of liked this woman's sense of humor. "The pig, not Coco. But maybe he'd take her too. She's awfully cute. Albeit a bit quick to jump to conclusions. And she's got a mean left hand."

"Ouch. She told me she slapped you."

"That's the first time that's ever happened. Hopefully the last."

"So, I've got a plan for fixing things with you two if you're interested."

Jesus, was he ever. He couldn't stop thinking about Coco and all the things they did together Friday night. He wanted to get to know her better and, well, spend a lot more time naked with her.

"Lady, I'm all ears."

The two talked for ten more minutes and organized the plan. When he got off the phone, he at least felt hopeful, which was a far cry from the despondency that had defined the past few days. It seemed a little crazy, but with a bit of luck, maybe it could work.

Chapter Fifteen

COCO put the finishing touches on her makeup, stood up, and tugged on her dress, which felt too short and was creeping up too far for her comfort level.

"Hurry, Coco, or we'll be late," Emma said, reaching for her purse.

"You sure I can't miss this altogether?"

Emma shook her head. "You owe it to these people to show up and thank them for what they did for you. You can pretend Elliott isn't there if that's what you'd prefer. Though I personally think you owe it to him—and to your relationship—to hear him out."

"We don't have a relationship. We had a hookup. One and done. Nothing more needs to be said."

Emma rolled her eyes. "You sure are a stubborn thing, I'll give you that."

Coco whacked her with her clutch purse.

Emma looked down at her boot-clad foot and her heel-clad one. "That looks super imbalanced. You want to Uber over there?"

"It's two blocks away. I will be fine. Besides, I need the exercise."

"After all that weight you lost in the wilderness, you need a good meal is what you need."

Coco made puppet motions with her fingers, like she was parroting whatever her friend had said to her.

They stepped out of her apartment and she hobbled down the steps and out the door to the fire station for the big search-and-rescue fundraiser.

When they arrived, they were lavished with attention. Everyone wanted to talk to Coco and find out how she was faring. The team of eight who'd found her in the mountains and ushered her out on the litter came by to greet her one by one, and Coco graciously thanked each of them for their heroic acts on her behalf.

She made a point to steer clear of Elliott, and he was honoring her wishes to keep his distance.

"You want a drink?" Emma said, heading toward the bar.

"Gin and tonic, two limes." Coco grabbed some sort of stuffed mushroom that was being passed by a waiter and popped it into her mouth. When Emma returned with drinks, she clinked her glass of wine up against Emma's glass. "Here's to being lost and then being found."

"I'll drink to that," Coco said. She looked around. "I thought you said there was some silent auction here we were to bid on."

Emma lifted her eyebrow, "Huh? Oh, it turns out it's a service auction. It's like people have offered up their services and interested parties will bid on it."

"Ahhh... gotcha. You mean a date auction? So, I could bid on one of these handsome mountaineering men to spend an evening with?"

"Yep." Emma took a sip of her wine. "Like that cute one over there. The one with the gorgeous eyes." She pointed toward Elliott.

Coco rolled her eyes and shook her head. "You don't let up, do you?"

Emma grinned. "That's why you pay me the big bucks." She toed the ground in front of them. "Speaking of big bucks… I took the liberty of signing you up for the auction."

"You what?" Coco's eyes widened.

"Well, I may not have mentioned this to you, but I do the accounting for the search-and-rescue organization and when one of my clients told me what they were doing, well, I thought it was a fun way to raise money and I knew you'd agree that it was the least you could do since they saved your life and all."

Coco glared. "It would have been nice had I known I was volunteering for this," she said through gritted teeth. "I'm not saying I wouldn't have done it but I don't appreciate going into this blind."

Emma waved her hand. "Sorry, Coco, didn't mean to leave you in the dark. It was kind of a last-minute thing. It'll be fun. I promise."

Coco sucked down her drink and hobbled over to get another one. No way could she do this without a buzz on.

Soon, a woman stepped onto the stage and welcomed the guests. She gave a little speech about all the good things the search-and-rescue group did and pointed out several guests in attendance who had also been rescued by them.

Coco blushed when they pointed her out and she lifted her hand tentatively in acknowledgment. She knew she should be standing up there thanking them and felt guilty for being annoyed with Emma for volunteering her. It was the least she could do. Now that she thought about it, she felt like an ungrateful little shit. These folks were nothing but wonderful to her. Even jerk-face over there, but that was another issue altogether.

Clearly she'd been caught up in her own idiocy a little much. She needed a dope slap of reality here. She was going to go up on that stage with a smile and ham it up and let the chips fall where they may. Even if she ended up on a date with a man old enough to be her great-grandpa.

Soon the auction began, and a succession of locals took turns walking to the stage to perform their philanthropic duties. She was almost glad she hadn't known about this in advance because there were women who'd dressed accordingly: one gal had on a bikini and a sash as if she were in a beauty competition. Another guy offered himself up for a date biking in the mountains and was dressed in a full Lycra biking kit. That sounded like a little slice of hell—did he know how steep those roads were?

Just as Coco's name was called, Emma grabbed her and whispered into her ear.

"Look. I spoke with Elliott. I was right. It was a stupid guy fantasy thing. He doesn't even know that woman, but he knew her name. He was fantasizing about you naked with her."

Coco curled her lip. "Really? Is this the right time for this conversation?"

Emma nodded in the direction of Elliott. "There's no time like the present, Coco. Now go get 'em." She gave her a little push toward the stage, leaving Coco to wonder if she should be weirded out or think it was kind of quaint that he fantasized about her like that.

She hobbled onto the stage, pointing down to her cast and rolling her eyes, and everyone laughed.

She spoke into the microphone.

"I would be remiss were I not to stand up here and thank you all to the depths of my heart for what you did for me. Let me tell you, being lost up there"—she pointed toward the mountains—"was not even remotely fun. It was scary as shit—" She made an "O" with her mouth and covered it with her hand. "Oops! Sorry! Any kids in the room? I will go wash my mouth out with soap as soon as I'm done and put a dollar in the swear jar as soon as I get one." Everyone laughed. She grabbed a sip of her drink and continued. "There were moments when I was certain I'd die out there. Especially when I started to think, truly think, about what a needle in a haystack you'd be searching for. I owe you all my life and I can never thank you enough. I hope it is sufficient for me to at least give one of you lucky folks a night with me, even though I'm not the wildest of dates these days." She pointed to her boot. "No running, no biking, and without a doubt, no hiking in the mountains." They all laughed.

At that point, the auctioneer started the bidding and several in the audience raised their bid cards. With the glare from the spotlight beaming on her, she had a hard time seeing what any of them looked like. People were bidding up by ten, twenty, even thirty dollars, but then someone announced, "I'd like to bid a thousand dollars."

The audience gasped.

And damned if she didn't know that voice. Because she'd heard it time and again in her memory over the past week, that voice whispering all the dirty things he'd wanted to do to her, and it made her breath hitch in her throat.

"I've got a thousand dollars. Do I have eleven hundred?"

It felt like the clock stopped completely as she waited to find out if someone would save her from a night alone with him.

"Going once, going twice, sold, to the man for one thousand dollars."

As Coco left the stage, she could see Emma practically giddy, jumping up and down and clapping her hands. No doubt about it: she was going to have to kill her.

Chapter Sixteen

COCO was silent as she sat next to Elliott as he drove with Oink secured in the dog crate on the back seat. She'd found a rancher outside of town willing to take in the pig. He promised he'd keep Oink and not turn her into dinner for ten, which was all Coco could ask for. So this was her official auction date: taking Oink to her forever home.

They arrived at the ranch and the man greeted them along with his wife and young children. There was a little girl who was about five and two boys younger than her. They squealed with joy when she took Oink out of the crate and she instantly knew her little piglet would be happy in her new surroundings, with three delightful siblings to care for her.

As they drove back home, Coco felt an ache in her chest. She'd miss that pig yet was glad about Oink's new home. There was no way she could have ever kept a pig.

"So, uh, if you're still looking for a kitten, someone dropped off a litter of tabby cats the other day. The orange kitties are always the nicest ones," she said. It was a date, after all, so she knew she needed some sort of small talk.

Elliott, who had also been awfully quiet, pursed his lips. "Maybe that would be a nice thing. Mom said she would be willing to take in a kitten."

"You want to go see them?"

He nodded. "Sure."

"There are three kittens to choose from. It's not exactly

the date with all the pussy you could want that you might have hoped for—"

He looked at her and blurted out a laugh. "You have got to be kidding me. Did you seriously just say that?"

She started laughing. "Well, rumor has it you did have your fantasies about a couple of pussies…"

He chucked her in the arm while trying to keep his eyes on the road. "Shut up, you!"

She rolled her eyes. "What?"

"That was just a thing. In my head. That slipped out when I got a little, well, excited."

She nodded. "Fair enough. I can appreciate your honesty with that. And I'm sorry I jumped to conclusions and clocked you in the face."

"You've got a mean left hand. I'd hate to see what would have happened if that had been a punch."

"Is there any way I can make it up to you?"

He reached over the gear shift and rested his hand on her thigh. "I don't suppose you have any interest in meeting Tammi…"

She raised her hand as if to slap him but then started laughing. "You are such a jerk! No, I'm not going to meet your fantasy neighbor. Though if you'll settle for this little kitty cat"—she pointed toward her crotch—"then I'm all yours."

At once, he did an illegal U-turn and headed down a different street in the direction of his house.

"Where you going?"

"Just going to pet a little pussy if that's okay with you."

She grinned and pulled his hand toward her lap. "Meow."

Thank you!

Thank you so much for reading **Lady Killer!** I hope you enjoyed it! If so, please help others find this book:

1. Help other people find this book by writing a review.

2. Sign up for my new releases email so you can find out about the next book as soon as it's available and get fun giveaways. http://eepurl.com/baaewn

3. Like my Facebook page. www.facebook.com/jennygardinerbooks

And I love to hear from readers! Let me know what you think about my books! You can write to me at jenny@jennygardiner.net, and visit me on the web at www.jennygardiner.net.

Up next: an all new series, starting with
Hard to Get.

Shrimply irresistible…

Lola Quigley can't believe her good luck when she wins a spot on the Food Channel's popular *Shop till you Drop*. The show features amateur foodies competing to produce a prize-winning meal from staples commonly found in food banks, where people often unload their most unwanted pantry items. Having lived on a near poverty-level budget for a few dark years when her life imploded unexpectedly, Lola had grown to love the challenge of creating delicious meals with the cheapest ingredients she could find on the sale shelf of the grocery store, or—in a twist of irony—donated from her local food bank. She just has to win this: the prize money would help her launch the soup kitchen food truck she's dreamed of starting. It'll be her way of paying it forward after she managed to dig out of a financial hole she'd doubted she ever *could* escape.

Levi Patton is pissed. He's stuck doing penance as a guest chef on an annoying cable reality TV show where overly enthusiastic wannabes try to outdo him with random undesirable ingredients. Will he ever get over the meteoric crash of his career after a food critic found the unmistakable tail of a rat floating atop his bouillabaisse at Levi's revered Washington, DC, restaurant? Convinced, but unable to prove, that a jealous sous chef sabotaged him, his name is now mud in the food world; he's drowning in the veritable toilet of the culinary industry: competing on *Shop till you Drop*. And he's totally screwed when he ends up pitted against the overly cheerful brunette with the tattoo of Popeye on her bicep, the very woman he'd left at the altar nearly a decade ago.

Read on for a sneak peek of *Hard to Get.*

Chapter One

LOLA Quigley's hands trembled against her keyboard as she opened the e-mail from the Food Channel that she'd been waiting months for. Before she opened it, she closed her eyes, sat back in her chair, rain her fingers through her long, brown hair, and then took in a deep, cleansing breath. If the response was negative, then oh well. She'd move on, and surely things would work out some other way. She reminded herself she needed to be at peace with whatever happened since it was all out of her control anyhow. Besides, after all she'd been through over the past handful of years, she'd find another way. She was tough and resilient, so she'd figure it out, one way or another. She always had.

She squinted her hazel eyes as her pointer finger hovered over her inbox before she finally clicked on the email and opened it up.

"It's only an email," she whispered like a mantra. "It's only an email." And then she drummed up the courage to actually read the damned thing.

Dear Miss Quigley,

Congratulations! You've been chosen to compete in an upcoming episode of Shop till you Drop*! Our producers loved your demo submission—especially when your cat jumped up on the table when you were eating your finished meal, which they thought was a charming touch. Especially when she started licking that corn smut and prickly pear soup you'd made—very creative side dish, by the way. And clearly delicious enough for a picky cat to enjoy. Please contact me at your earliest convenience and I'll provide details. We're excited to have you on the show!*

Best,
Amy Ming, Producer

Lola sat for a moment staring in disbelief at what she'd just read. She had been selected as a competitor on one of the most popular cooking shows in the country, in which home cooks raced the clock and each other to shop for and create a prize-winning meal using non-perishable items cast-off from food donated to food banks.

The tall, athletically-built brunette knew she had her work cut out for her, but she'd been preparing for this for years, like it or not. Plenty of times since things went so wrong, back when that jerk Levi did what he did, she'd gotten by on the kindness of donations from food banks and church food pantries. And yeah, a lot of times what was donated were ingredients that perhaps seemed aspirational when the donor purchased them. She was good at making something from nothing. Like when she found in her donation bag a box of make-it-yourself German spaetzle, red curry paste, fish oil, a bag of pork rinds, and a jar of deviled eggs. She turned it into a makeshift German/Thai carbonara-esque dish that didn't taste half bad after she'd worked her magic.

And now that she'd pulled herself from the pit of despair, where she'd been languishing for far too long, now that she could even splurge every now and again for a half-decent meal out, she was going to test that rumbling-belly-what-am-I-gonna-eat muscle memory so that she could win the hundred thousand dollar prize and the chance to pay it forward by launching a mobile soup kitchen to feed those in the community who struggled to feed themselves.

Now that she'd gotten this far, she just had to win. Whatever it was going to take, she'd do it. She was going to make darn good and sure that the legacy of Levi leaving her at the altar, ultimately so distraught she dropped out of school and then failed at a succession of low-paying jobs for years, was going to be one of vindication. This phoenix's rise from the ashes would be one for the ages, because she was going to win *Shop till You Drop* come hell or high water.

Chapter Two

SOMETIMES Levi Patton indulged his less noble side, wondering what he'd done to deserve seeing his life's work swirling down the crapper in one epic flush.

Because boy, had his career done a sudden one-eighty, going from meteoric success as the boy-genius on the DC food scene to the culinary equivalent of a fifteen-car-pileup on the interstate, after the vaunted food critic for the Washington Chronicle encountered an unmistakable piece of a rat's tail floating in his Bouillabaisse.

Holy crap, was that a bad day in his life. He'd suspected that the man seated at the table by the window had been the much-anticipated undercover food critic, and had alerted his staff to take care to ensure that his meal was perfect. He oversaw each dish as it left the kitchen, which was why he knew there hadn't been a rat body part that had randomly found its way into his fine French fusion cuisine when it left the kitchen. Someone had sabotaged him, and he had a good idea who it was, but had never been able to prove it.

Rumor had it the critic at first thought it was simply an antenna from the langoustine lobster that had fallen into the broth. Butt upon further inspection, there was no doubt that it was, indeed, a rodent tail, complete with a core layer of bone covered by that telltale hairless, circular-ridged skin. Whoever had it out for Levi knew what he was doing, no question about that.

His demise was fast and painful. He quickly lost a restaurant he'd worked years to finally open only months earlier, to rave reviews. But worse still, he lost his reputation, and he'd forever be known as Rat-Boy, the moniker the tabloids found it cute to dub him.

Levi pressed the heels of his hands to his brown eyes, trying to massage the stress of his life away, to no avail. He sat down at the makeshift desk he'd set up in the living room of his mostly empty efficiency apartment, and switched on his computer. He then tried to massage his weary scalp by pressing his fingers through his wavy brown hair, but even that didn't help. It seemed the headache that had overtaken him months ago had parked itself in his brain and wasn't planning to depart any time soon.

What had he done to deserve this? Well, at least this in particular? Nothing, really, Had he made some poor decisions in his life, maybe some that led to him hurting people who didn't deserve it? Yep. No doubt about it. In fact, there were likely people who thought he was the worst person to walk the face of the earth. Like, say, Lola Quigley, his high school sweetheart who he'd planned to meet at the justice of the peace to get married way back when they were young and stupid. The very Lola he blew off, for reasons not even worth mulling over at this point.

And while yeah, that was about the shittiest thing he could have done, the fact was he was a kid. And he screwed up. And he'd sent about a bazillion letters (not to mention e-mails and text messages) of apology—since all of his calls went unanswered. Eventually he stopped trying to persuade Lola that he wasn't a flaming asshole. Because even he knew that deep down, he had to have been in order to have committed such a hurtful act. Even if it was to save his own self, which was why he did it, it cost Lola dearly, emotionally, and no doubt cost her her self-esteem as well.

Levi rubbed his eyes again. If he had a dollar for every time he'd gone over this in his brain… Yet a whole lotta good it would do him. He scrolled through his emails, seeing if he had gotten any responses to the many job applications he'd submitted. Nothing popped out at him, until he saw something that said it was from the Food Channel. No doubt some investigative reporter wanting to humiliate him even more.

Instead, he found an email from a producer, the contents of which were rather curious.

Greetings—

I am the producer of the popular Shop till you Drop *show in which home cooks compete to for prize money by making meals with some of the unusual foods donated to food banks. Normally we pit home cooks against one another, but in light of your unfortunate circumstances, we thought it might be interesting to give you a chance to demonstrate your culinary skills against top-tier home cooks, and see what might unfold. I hope you'll consider this opportunity to join us in this adventure. I think it could go a long way toward rehabilitating your faltering career and give America the chance to forgive you. I look forward to your reply.*

Best,

Amy Ming, Producer

Amy Ming. Why did that name ring a bell? Amy Ming. Ming. Ming. Ming. He held up his finger. She'd been a newly-hired line-cook at his restaurant, hadn't she? It was like her third week on the job when it all went to crap. Why on earth would she want anything to do with him? Was she going to try to shame him on national television?

He shook his head. *Nah.* She seemed like too nice of a woman to do that. Weird she'd reach out to him like this, but maybe she had her reasons. Maybe she could help him solve the mystery of what happened that night. At this point, what could it hurt for him to go on there? It's not as if he would embarrass himself! And not like he was going to have an issue with his competition. Sure, maybe they'll want to outdo him. And maybe he'd go easy on them, at least at first. Hopefully even if they did recognize him as the Rat-Boy, they'd take a little pity on him, cut him some slack, and give him a tiny chance for redemption.

It was a long shot, for sure. But what he needed was a hail-Mary pass right now, so like it or not, he was going to stand tall and cook his ass off. And win the prize, enough to at least dig him out of some of the financial hole he'd found himself in.

Okay, Amy Ming, Producer. You're on. Bring it, baby.

~ * ~

Hard to Get – June 2020

About Jenny

Jenny Gardiner is the author of #1 Kindle Bestseller *Slim to None* and the award-winning novel *Sleeping with Ward Cleaver*. Her latest works are the *It's Reigning Men* series, the *Royal Romeos* series, the *Falling for Mr. Wrong* series, the *Chick Magnet* series and her new *Hard to Get* series. She also published the memoir *Winging It: A Memoir of Caring for a Vengeful Parrot Who's Determined to Kill Me,* now re-titled *Bite Me: a Parrot, a Family and a Whole Lot of Flesh Wounds*; the novels *Anywhere but Here*; *Where the Heart Is*; the essay collection *Naked Man on Main Street*, and *Accidentally on Purpose* and *Compromising Positions* (writing as Erin Delany); and is a contributor to the humorous dog anthology *I'm Not the Biggest Bitch in This Relationship*.

Her work has been found in Ladies Home Journal, the Washington Post, Marie-Claire.com, and on NPR's Day to Day. She was also a columnist for Charlottesville's Daily Progress for over a decade, a food writer for Cville Weekly, and the Volunteer Coordinator for the Virginia Film Festival for the past nine years.

She has worked as a professional photographer, an orthodontic assistant (learning quite readily that she was not cut out for a career in polyester), a waitress (probably her highest-paying job), a TV reporter, a pre-obituary writer, as well as a publicist to a United States Senator (where she first learned to write fiction). She's photographed Prince Charles (and her assistant husband got him to chuckle!), Elizabeth Taylor, and the president of Uganda. She and her husband and a menagerie of pets now live a less exotic life in Virginia.

Visit Jenny at her website jennygardiner.net and sign up for her newsletter, her blog, or find her on Facebook and Twitter. And every blue moon she'll post adorable pictures of her pets on Instagram as @thejennygardiner.